Praise for
Deadly Gamble

I loved Deadly Gamble! If you love historical cozy mystery books, I highly recommend that you read the book! The exciting plot, well-written characters, and beautifully detailed descriptions make this a must-read!
Christy's Cozy Corners

Deadly Gamble is a riveting story of spies and intrigue in a city trying to hold on to its luster.
Cozy Up With Kathy

Deadly Gamble is an enjoyable story with great characters, a well-plotted mystery, and realistic actions.
Carla Loves To Read

Historical fiction, murder, and lovely characters. Parker provides the backdrop and her characters are well-developed. For anyone who likes cozy mysteries or WWII fiction, will enjoy this book.
Christa Reads and Writes

Also from Kate Parker

The Deadly Series
Deadly Scandal
Deadly Wedding
Deadly Fashion
Deadly Deception
Deadly Travel
Deadly Darkness
Deadly Cypher
Deadly Broadcast
Deadly Rescue
Deadly Manor
Deadly Gamble
Deadly Performance

The Victorian Bookshop Mysteries
The Vanishing Thief
The Counterfeit Lady
The Royal Assassin
The Conspiring Woman
The Detecting Duchess

The Milliner Mysteries
The Killing at Kaldaire House
Murder at the Marlowe Club

The Mystery at Chadwick House

Deadly Performance

Kate Parker

JDP Press

This is a work of fiction. All names, characters, and incidents are products of the author's imagination. Any resemblance to actual occurrences or persons, living or dead, is coincidental. Historical events and personages are fictionalized.

Deadly Performance

Copyright ©2024 by Kate Parker

All rights reserved. With the exception of brief quotes used in critical articles or reviews, no part of this book may be reproduced in any form or by any means without written permission of the author.

ISBN: 979-8-9920152-0-1 (ebook)

ISBN: 979-8-9920152-1-8 (print)

Published by JDP Press

Cover Design by Lyndsey Lewellen of Llewellen Designs

Dedication

For my family, my friends, and anyone who enjoys a good historical mystery.

To John, forever.

London, late June, 1941

Chapter One

Dear Esther,

I'm dreaming of murdering my father. Most of the time I use a hatchet. Please may I visit this weekend and dream of something pleasant?

It's been over a month since I've seen Adam and I'm going mad. The army only let him come home because we were bombed out and he wanted to know if anything was salvageable. Of course, nothing was.

Now that the Germans have stopped bombing London for the moment, I wish I could say life is getting back to normal, but rationing is getting worse and there's no housing available. I'll be forced to live with my father until they send me to prison for killing him.

My father is treating me with frosty disdain if he even acknowledges my presence. Dinnertime is the worst of it. We both eat in silence except for requests to pass the salt. I'm dying for someone intelligent to talk to.

I can tell my father is sorry I had to move home. Fortunately, he knows if I leave, he'll be urged to take on a family who's been bombed out. Better the devil you know…

Your father suggested I write and arrange a visit, as he is tired of me snapping at everyone at the newspaper and even someone as powerful as he is can't convince the army to arrange leave for Adam or find me somewhere else to live.

Please say yes. I'll come out Friday night and return Sunday night. I'll wash dishes, play with my two favorite people, anything if I can bribe you to give me a reprieve from my father. I do believe a baby would be less work than he is, always having to tiptoe around so as not to disturb him.

How are Johnny and Rebecca? I'm sure they're growing as though they are weeds. Give them a kiss for me and tell them Aunty Livvy would love to see them.

Please send word and invite me before my dreams come true and I take a hatchet to my father. Your loving friend,

Livvy

The next afternoon, Esther called me at the newspaper, laughing at my hysterics and telling me she'd love for me to visit.

So it was on Friday, immediately after I finished at the *Daily Premier* for the day, that I caught a train to Oxford and then the bus to the pretty Cotswold village where Esther lived. Her Victorian vicarage was a large, two-story honey-colored stone house with a pitched roof on the edge of the village next to a magnificent stone church. The tiny front garden held mounds of flowering bushes and lazily buzzing bees. I arrived to a loud and enthusiastic greeting from Johnny and Rebecca before their nurserymaid took them off for their baths while Esther and I had a dinner of seasoned vegetable marrows mixed in a casserole with stale bread crumbs.

I don't know how Esther's cook did it, but she had prepared a delicious main dish. She paired it with a fresh green salad straight from their garden. I couldn't remember eating anything that good since rationing started.

"You are a lifesaver," I began.

"You are too dramatic," Esther replied.

"Food worth the effort to eat it."

"My father needs to find you a job covering theater performances. All that flamboyance needs an outlet. That's what our headmistress at St. Agnes said."

"I'm not flamboyant. I'm dull, boring."

"I shared your letter with my father. We both laughed until we cried."

After we ate, I followed Esther up the narrow stairs to the nursery to say good night to her children and listen to the bedtime story before we sat in the drawing room with our herb tea and talked.

"Be honest with me. Is it just your father who has been bothering you, or is there more to it than that?" Esther asked, tucking her feet under her on the big, stuffed chair.

"Well, I miss Adam."

"I miss James. We all have that problem."

She was right. James was away who knew where with the army, the same as Adam. "Your father had the sense to set you and your household up in a relatively safe village in a nice house."

"He knew he didn't want me and the children living with him if our house was bombed," Esther said with a slight smile.

"At least he made plans in advance." A little of my disgust came out in my tone.

"He had the money to buy this place and fix it up before the war," Esther told me, "unlike your father, who has a government position with a government salary."

"I wish he understood I have no choice but to live with him."

"He can't be that bad."

"You've always liked my father," I grumbled. It was true. Just as I had a soft spot for her father, bold, outspoken Sir Henry, Esther enjoyed the company of my reserved, quiet father. I finished my cup of tea and poured more from the pot.

"Sir Ronald isn't so bad."

"You don't have to live with him." I realized I was snapping at her and held up my hands. "I might do better putting up with him if we had a cook as talented as yours."

"Tomorrow, I'm putting you to work in the kitchen garden so you can appreciate how much work goes into having tasty vegetables and herb tea."

"I'll be glad to help you, but unfortunately, my father's back garden isn't big enough to grow much of anything. And while Mrs. Johnson tries to cook us decent dinners, they certainly aren't as good as tonight's."

Esther leaned forward, concern written across her face.

"Come on, Livvy. This isn't the person I know. If you don't care for something, you find a way to change it. But you're not learning to cook. You're not attempting to find another home. What is really wrong?"

"I don't know." I shrugged. "I haven't felt well in a couple of weeks."

"I thought you weren't in London the night your flat was destroyed."

"I wasn't. I was at Abby's. It saved my life. Several of my neighbors were killed while they were sheltering in the cellar when the building collapsed on them."

"How awful." Her eyes widened. "Do you feel guilty?"

"No. The bombing is so…random. And for the first few weeks, I was busy replacing what I could. Dresses. Shoes. Hats. An umbrella. I had Adam with me for a few days and it was so nice having him around. Reassuring me. And then time seemed to start to drag. Nothing changed from one day to the next."

"You're bored." Esther nodded sagely.

"Does being bored make you listless? Does it make you sleep more? Does it make your insides ache?"

"Perhaps you're depressed. There is so much of it about. After a while, this war gets to everyone."

"Living with my father would make anyone depressed."

"What do you want to do?"

"Stop living with my father. End rationing. End the war."

Esther nodded. "I want the threat of invasion to go away."

"Oh." I set down my teacup and leaned forward as if to invite her into a conspiracy. "There's talk that if Hitler doesn't invade in the next few weeks, he'll miss his chance. Tides and storms and typical English weather will make landing on our coast difficult for an invasion. And then, there are rumors that the Germans are about to invade Russia, instead of us."

"Does my father know all this?" Esther asked.

"Of course. Sir Henry keeps track of every move by every army, particularly so he can be careful not to print anything he shouldn't."

"I wish he'd tell me. All he does when he calls or visits is ask about his grandchildren." Her shoulders sagged.

"At least he's interested. If I ever have children, I am certain my father will never show any interest." Of that I had no doubt.

If I let him live that long.

No, I knew he was in no danger. I was too listless and miserable for committing murder.

Chapter Two

As soon as I arrived at work on Monday morning, rested from my weekend in the country visiting Esther and the children, the phone by my desk at the *Daily Premier* rang. I picked it up and said "Mrs. Redmond" with no inflection.

"Esther said you were grumpy," Sir Henry's voice boomed out of the receiver. "I can't do anything about Adam and the army, and I can't do anything about the Germans blowing up your block of flats, but I can make your job more intriguing. Come up to my office."

The line went dead.

What was it this time? I was being parachuted into occupied France to meet with the Resistance. I was being sent to Shetland in the far north to ride the Shetland bus to Norway to see the fight against the Nazis on skis. I was being sent by air to Cairo to send stories back about life for our troops in North Africa. My imagination ran wild the whole way upstairs to Sir Henry's office. He, and the spymaster Sir Malcolm Freemantle, were the men who could make my fantasies a reality.

If they weren't giving me assignments that made my reality a nightmare.

His secretary nodded me toward the door behind her and I walked over, knocked on the door, and went in.

Sir Henry held up a hand, the other holding the receiver, as he said, "I'm sure she'll be perfect for what you want. Her style is rather—exuberant. Yes, she's available immediately."

I wondered if he meant me. Exuberant? No one had called me that in a long time.

He laughed and said, "Always happy to help a friend." When he hung up, he waved for me to approach his desk and take a chair. A chair from where I had to look up, since Sir Henry kept his on a platform to compensate for his short stature.

I sat and said, "You wanted to see me, Sir Henry?"

"Yes. *The Stage* weekly newspaper is in need of a columnist to write reviews—well, not really reviews. Their previous person has been picked up by the MOD to produce entertainment for the troops."

So much for any travel or excitement. Or being of any use for our country. Unlike the man reporting to the Ministry of Defense whose place I was taking, I wouldn't be doing anything for the war effort. "What are reviews that aren't really reviews?"

"A synopsis of the plot or a mention of the various skits in a variety show plus mentioning all the performers, with special mention of those who do an excellent job. *The Stage* is a weekly, so you'll only cover two to three shows for each edition, plus news bits about touring productions, MOD shows, how rationing affects theater productions and performers, and so on."

First, the important points. "Who's paying my salary?"

"I am, since you are only on loan to them. Same salary as before."

My sigh of relief was audible. "Where are their offices?"

"Bush House. Just down the street on Aldwych."

At least it wasn't Canterbury or Cambridge. On second thought, that would get me out of my father's home. Aloud I said, "I'm surprised they're letting them use up newsprint for such a niche subject. Paper is as rationed as the next thing."

"That 'niche subject,' as you call it, is entertaining the troops as well as civilians and keeping us all from losing our minds. They have to have a way to organize their various productions, get the word out on hiring, that sort of thing. And nothing gets the word out the same way as a good press campaign." Sir Henry stared at me. "When was the last time you went to the theater?"

"Not in ages, but I've rather lost my taste for frivolity."

"And here you used to be the most dramatic young lady I knew." He smiled at me then. "Give it a try, Livvy. Get some life back into you. Esther says you've been down at the mouth since the Germans bombed your flat. True?"

I gave off a deep sigh. "Probably."

"Seen too much of the war?"

"I feel as if I'm not pulling my weight. And I see Esther with two children, and I've not even started."

"When did you last see Adam?"

"Two weeks after the flat exploded."

Sir Henry shook his head, biting back a smile. "I think a lot of people want to see the war end, if only for that reason."

"Because I was bombed out of my flat?"

"Procreation."

I could feel color creeping up my face. Sir Henry cleared his throat, embarrassed by his outspokenness in front of a young lady, a friend of his daughter's. He turned his face away a little.

"How are Johnny and Rebecca?" he asked. Nothing could wipe the smile off his face when he mentioned Esther's children.

"Your grandchildren are perfect. I spent the weekend with Esther, helping to weed the garden. It was a terrific break, but now I'm back here in reality again."

"If you lived there, that would be your reality. But the question is, are you back to chewing people's necks and snapping their bones? None of us deserve your bad temper, Livvy."

"I'm sorry. I've just been feeling run down. Spending a weekend around Esther and away from my father was helpful."

"Good. I want you showing enthusiasm for this assignment, because I've selected you for this position especially. You gave the most vibrant and exciting performances in the school plays at St. Agnes."

"This is the professional theater. They won't care about my time in school plays."

"But you'll understand what is going on."

"All right. When do I start this new assignment, what are the hours, and so on?" If it would let me avoid my father, I might begin to show enthusiasm.

"You start immediately. The paper comes out on Thursdays and the working week for the theater, or your part of it, starts Tuesday, so you have Sunday and Monday off. Of course, that can be rearranged as needed. Your hours will be eleven or noon until seven or eight on performance days so you can get home before the blackout starts. If you're still there in the autumn, the hours will shift earlier because of the blackout."

"And if Adam gets leave?"

"You'll know when that is ahead of time?"

"A little."

"Then double up on your so-called reviews and anything else before he hits town. Then you'll be free when he's here. Couldn't be simpler." Sir Henry seemed to have an answer for everything.

"Well, then, let's give it a try." It might be interesting, if useless for winning a war.

"Go see Simon Chapell. He's the editor of *The Stage*. He'll show you what needs to be done. He's in the office now."

I went downstairs, packed up my things, and walked up the road to Bush House. Most of the building, which was made of white stone and had two statues of people in ancient dress over the doorway, was in use by the BBC, which made the place appropriate for them. *The Stage* had a few rooms on the first floor. No one challenged me as I climbed the stairs and walked into their offices.

As soon as I met him, I knew why Simon and Sir Henry got on so well. They were the same height. Men who wanted to be judged by the fight of their words in print and their management style, not their physical appearance. I heard a trace of Newcastle in his speech, just as I did in Sir Henry's.

Simon "Call me Si" Chapell had a rubbery face, a nearly bald head, and a glaring waistcoat of printed red silk. After shaking hands, he showed me to my desk just outside his cupboard-size office. The space was too small to allow clutter and papers to swamp our rooms, although it was a close-run thing.

"I've never covered stories such as these before," I told him.

"Sir Henry wouldn't have sent you if he didn't think you were up to the job. Go out, take notes, come back, type it up. Couldn't be easier. Do you know anything about the theater?"

"I've attended theater productions and I've performed in school plays. Not much of a background, is it?" I admitted.

"Did you enjoy it? Watching and acting?"

"Yes."

A broad smile crossed his face. "Good. That's all you need. I was an actor once. Not very good." He laughed. "Horrible, in fact. But I loved it, and that's all I needed to run *The Stage*."

He picked up a couple of show bills. "Let's make the rounds of the variety stages today, or at least make a start.

Introduce you around. Ready?"

I gave him a weak smile. "Always."

We visited three theaters before the opening of that day's performances. I was first introduced to the chairman at each theater, a sort of master of ceremonies, producer, and director of the show, all rolled into one. They were each brash, charming, and loud. Their shows were similar in that each had scantily clad female dancers, loud, mildly amusing comedians, singers of patriotic tunes, and musicians playing both patriotic tunes and lively dance music.

No doubt they cheered up their audiences. They bored me to tears. How long had it been since they started to bore me? When had I become so old and jaded?

After we left the third theater, Si asked, "What do you think?"

"I think I'd rather cover the plays. I'm more familiar with that."

"Don't tell me you don't appreciate all those chorus girls in their costumes?" He wiggled his eyebrows.

I shrugged. "I prefer plays to singing and dancing."

"Tomorrow we'll go to a couple of the theaters where they are rehearsing plays that will open in the next week or two. We'll have you take notes and then write them up when we get back."

That sounded more in line with what my job should be. "I've heard there's a new Noel Coward play coming to one of the theaters."

"The Piccadilly. You're a Coward fan, are you? Then you'll

enjoy *Blithe Spirit*. We'll start there tomorrow."

Si was right. I loved *Blithe Spirit*.

With the exception of Shakespeare, most of the plays on the London stages were comedies. There were also ballets and operas for those who wanted something more cultural to take their minds off the war and the destruction just outside the theater doors, but comedies were the most popular. Well, after variety shows.

After Si had spent two weeks taking me around to every theater in London and introduced me as the new reporter and reviewer to every chairman and producer, he let me loose the next day to make the rounds of Haymarket, Shaftsbury Avenue, and Piccadilly Circus. I had been to two theaters already, out in the sun and heat of a particularly bright and stifling early July Wednesday, before I went to the smallish, perhaps seven hundred seat, Regent Theatre.

The white stone, columned exterior was similar to other theaters in the area. The marquee listed the play at the Regent as a comedy in rehearsals called *Have You Seen My Mother-in-Law?* The company performing it had already spent a year on tour all over England to good reviews. I expected to be given the usual press words, "Already a success in other cities, now we expect a long and enthusiastic run at the Regent, grand old theater, the play starring fan favorites..." and be sent on my way.

The box office was closed, so I went around the side to an alley that led to the stage door. The door was propped open, another sign that the same as all old theaters, the

Regent broiled inside on a sunny summer day.

I walked in and waited until my eyes adjusted to the darkness inside. A figure burst out of the darkness and shoved me aside to get past and outside. I was spun around and saw by the figure's outline in the doorway that he was a man of above average height and muscular build.

A gravelly voice behind me barked out, "Who are you? State your business."

I turned around again and found myself facing a skinny old man. "I'm with *The Stage*. I'm supposed to see the producer to find out if he wants me to put anything in this week's issue. I understand the first performance is on Friday."

"He's on the stage with the others. Waiting for the ambulance."

Ambulance? Not something you expected during a rehearsal. My fingers itched to pull out my notebook. "You sent that man to summon the ambulance?" I asked. That explained why he was in too much of a hurry for good manners.

"What man?"

"The man who almost knocked me over."

"There was no man here. We telephoned. I'm Old Nick. Stage doorman." He gestured me on into the gloom with an air of boredom.

I walked down the hall, listening for voices, until the space suddenly widened out into the backstage area. From there, I followed the voices and the stage lighting until I found myself on the edge of the stage.

Everyone, actors and craft, was standing around on stage staring at one pale young woman writhing around on the floor and tangling herself in a square of dusty carpet. At least the stage was well-lit, so it was easy to see she'd injured her leg. I didn't see any blood. A couple of men I assumed were stagehands knelt at her side, reassuring her.

"What happened?" I asked an older woman who moved over to stand near me.

"They were rehearsing a dance scene in the first act when the carpet slipped. It's a fast jive dance and her legs went out from under her, poor dear."

"Couldn't they have tacked it down so it wouldn't slip? It's just painted wooden floor underneath," I asked.

"The stagehands were told to do that, and they swear they did." The woman was in regular clothes without stage makeup, but I was certain she was an actress. There was something about her speaking voice and the way she carried herself. "I'm Marnie Keller. I play the mother-in-law in this farce."

Marnie Keller was a well-known comedienne, but I'd never seen her close up before. She was shorter than I'd pictured her. "I'm Olivia Redmond. From *The Stage*."

"Are you responsible for 'Chit Chat'?"

"I've been taking over that column for the last week or so." "Chit Chat" featured news and gossip from the London stage, and there were certainly plenty of people willing to give me suggestions.

"I knew there'd been a change. Si's a lovely man, but he favors his favorites in the coverage. You don't do that."

"I don't have any favorites. I don't know anybody," I said with a shrug. "Who's the young lady on the floor?"

"Wanda Thomas. She plays one of my daughters."

As I jotted down her name, the ambulance crew arrived to take her to the hospital. I made sure to find out which one she was being taken to. "Why did you call the play a farce? It's billed as a comedy."

"Since we've come to London, we've had costumes shredded and things stolen. Personal things disappearing from our dressing rooms. None of this happened when we were on tour. The whole show since we arrived in London has been one big farce." Marnie shook her head as she watched Wanda being loaded onto a stretcher. "This should never have happened."

Chapter Three

"Were the things that were stolen valuable?" I asked Marnie.

"I lost a little gold locket on a chain that I wear in every performance as a good luck charm. There was a lucky rabbit's foot that vanished. And a meat pie that was to be someone's lunch yesterday disappeared."

"Definitely valuable," I agreed. "No idea who's taking things?"

"No, nor who shredded the costumes. They aren't easy to come by with clothing rationing. It affects us more than most people, since a lot of what we wear onstage we wouldn't be caught dead in offstage."

"Can you borrow from other companies?"

"Some. People have been kind. Then our costumers, our seamstresses, have to work twice as hard to make things fit right or create something new," Marnie told me. For a star, she seemed well informed on how everything in the theater worked. When I told her so, she laughed. "I've only been doing this my entire life."

"Who are you?" boomed at me.

I jumped, but Marnie didn't blink. "The new girl from *The*

Stage. Olivia Redmond."

"I've come to find out if the producer has anything he wants to put into this week's edition. May I put in about Wanda Thomas injuring her leg and going to hospital?" I asked as I turned around.

"Only in a little box so it doesn't look as if it happened here. Ian Nelson, producer." He held out his hand. He was pale, with a wide face and a well-pressed suit. As we shook hands, I noticed his nails were buffed to a shine and his skin uncalloused.

"Hey," said a burly middle-aged man on his hands and knees checking the rug and floor now that Wanda had been wheeled away. "There's no sign of those tacks, although you can see the pinholes in the floor. Our thief has stolen those, too."

"Nonsense. You're just trying to cover up for your carelessness," Nelson said, blotting his handkerchief on his broad forehead that had apparently spread to his crown over the years.

"That's our head stagehand, Gil Baker," Marnie told me in a low voice, gesturing to the large man peering closely at the floor. "He's a good guy. Conscientious. But the producer doesn't want to believe him."

"Why?" I still didn't understand all the complex relationships in the theater.

"Oh, you're green." Marnie shook her head. "The producer produces the play, finds the backers to put in money, and if it doesn't go on stage on time, he loses their money and won't be able to get any more out of them. The building owner doesn't make money when the stage is sitting idle, including when rehearsals are being held, so the owner is going to complain to the producer he's costing him money. The producer, being blamed on all sides, needs someone else to blame."

"What do you think happened?" I asked.

"Our stagehands seem to know what they're doing. I have worked in this theater before with these men and they're a good bunch." Marnie watched the argument build for a minute. "Any hotter and you won't be able to understand a word the stagehand says with his Cockney accent."

Indeed, the two men facing off on stage could have been performing. It needed only an audience in the seats. Marnie was right about the stagehand's accent; as the argument progressed, I could only make out every other word.

Nelson, the producer, either could understand him or didn't care what he said. He was convinced the stagehand had failed to properly secure the rug. He finally put up his hand, palm out, and walked away toward me. Marnie gave me a big smile.

"We'll need a casting call to replace Betty in this week's issue," the producer said as he reached me offstage.

"Who?" I asked.

"Wanda's part. Si will know what to put in. I spoke to the ambulance crew and they think Wanda broke her leg," Nelson told me.

"Can we get back to work, please? We'll start from just after the dance." The tall, thin man who shouted this walked out on stage holding a bright red mug. "You, there, read Betty's lines for the rest of this scene."

I looked up from my notebook where I'd been making notes to realize he was waving a script in my direction. Despite being nearly sixty or so, he was handsome with silver hair and dark eyes.

"Well, don't keep him waiting," Marnie said. "Go on."

"Who is he?"

"Marshall Lowe, our director. He needs someone to read her lines so we can rehearse. Go on. Break a leg."

"Someone just did," I murmured. I'd never even seen the script before. This would be painful for everyone to hear. I walked onto the stage and looked out into the auditorium. The vast space, full of chairs that would hold people Friday night, frightened me.

Certainly larger than the auditorium at St. Agnes. I turned back and looked at the director.

"Stand on that X there," he said, pointing to a mark on the floor, "and read the lines marked 'Betty.' Don't do any of the movements." He slapped a script in my hand that had Betty's lines underlined.

I nodded as two men stepped onto the stage without scripts. One of them, shorter and darker haired, said, "I'm Robbie Day, playing the vicar. He's Bud Cosby, playing Frank. And you're the new reporter from *The Stage?* Please remember our names when you review this—"

"Start with 'Golly, that was fun.'" Marshall Lowe interrupted him as he stepped to the side of the stage, not giving me time to write down their names.

I looked down and realized that was my line. "Golly, that was fun. We should go dancing every night." I tried projecting my voice past the stage without tripping over my tongue and just about managed it.

The two men made saying their lines effortless.

Lowe interrupted them occasionally to make changes in where they stood or how they said their lines. He ignored me, which hurt. When we finished the scene and went on to another that didn't involve Betty, he didn't even say "Thank you."

The producer waved to me.

I stepped to the back of the stage where Nelson stood. "Well done, Miss…"

"Mrs. Redmond. *The Stage* weekly."

"Oh, I remembered the newspaper, just not your name. Come up to my office and we'll sort out the ads that need to go in for tomorrow's edition. Otherwise, they'll do us no good. No good indeed."

Before we could go anywhere, a thin young man in dire need of a shave and in a ratty-looking suit that was too large for him burst onto the stage. I thought for a moment he was one of the actors and this was part of the play until Lowe, the director, shouted, "What are you doing here?"

The young man walked over and stood inches from his face. "I'm here to see my play produced. *My* play."

"That's all we need," Nelson muttered. "Philip Bernard. The playwright. Or not." Then he looked at me and said, "You didn't hear that."

I nodded as I continued to watch the two men.

"I told you, we can't. This isn't your play. Nothing but Shakespeare or comedies until the war ends," Lowe told him.

"So, you made my play a comedy. Do you think having your mother murdered is funny?" Bernard shouted. He sounded hysterical more than angry.

"No, but—"

"You took the biggest tragedy of my life and made it a comedy so audiences can laugh at me."

"No, Philip. No one is laughing at you. This isn't your play. Now, get off the stage. We have work to do," Lowe said, his voice displaying his lack of patience.

While the drama continued on stage, Nelson the producer led me around the stage and into the audience. We walked most of the way up the aisle until he gestured me to sit in a row. I slid across three red velvet seats, which were looking a little worn, while Nelson sat on the aisle seat.

"Welcome to my preferred office," he told me.

He quickly worked out the wording for the notice on Wanda Thomas' accident and then the ad for her replacement while I continued to watch the unscripted drama onstage. The young man in the too-large suit took a swing at the director, who easily ducked the punch. The director, despite being thirty years older than the playwright, ducked the next punch as well before landing one of his own, sending the young man to the floor.

By that time, the stagehands had separated the two men. "Now, get off of my stage," the director shouted. The young man slunk off, saying something I didn't hear.

"Will you be reviewing the play in this week's issue?" the producer asked, having ignored the fight on stage.

"Not unless I get a chance to see it through without any accidents," I told him. "Do the stagehands need to double as bouncers in many theaters?"

"No. Most theaters don't have obnoxious directors such as Marshall Lowe aggravating cast and crew to the point of fisticuffs."

"Did you have to hire extra crew for bouncers for this play?"

"Good heavens, no. I'm of the 'Let Lowe solve his own problems' school. But I think you should tell your reading public about saving the play by playing Betty in rehearsals," Nelson said, a twinkle in his eye.

"I hardly played her. I merely read out her lines so the rehearsal could go ahead," I told him. I was under no delusion that I was really acting, or that I was any good.

"For a spur of the moment reading, you did well." Nelson rose and said, "May I please request that you get that ad in for this week's edition." He didn't make it sound as if it was a question or a request as he handed me his copy.

I moved out into the aisle behind him. "I think I have enough time to get these both in for this week. Good luck, Mr. Nelson."

"No!" He looked horrified. "It's 'Break a leg,' Mrs. Redmond."

I went back out through the stage door, the front door being locked this time of day, but the stage doorman, Old Nick, was nowhere to be seen.

Si was in his office when I arrived back at Bush House and he sat in a sort of anticipated glee while I told the story of Wanda Thomas's bad luck.

"She does have a broken leg. I verified that with the hospital on my way back here. We need to get that notice and the ad for her replacement in the paper," I told him.

"Too bad we don't have time to add it in," Si told me with a contented smile.

"You said our deadline is tomorrow morning. Why the sudden change?" I asked.

"Then you'll have to change the copy at the printer to include his notices. I won't go across the street to help Marshall Lowe." Si set his rubbery features in a glower. When I asked why, he refused to say another word.

Our office descended into silence. It sounded the same as dinnertime in my father's house.

Chapter Four

My brief moment of glory on a West End stage filled my next letter to Adam, but didn't cause a ripple in the rest of England. The next morning, I reached the printer's shop early to find it was in an area that had been battered in the Blitz. Up and down the street, shopkeepers were cleaning away rubble, replacing broken glass, and here and there, a new building was slowly rising in one of the many vacant lots left by the Luftwaffe. The printer's shop had its front window replaced with a wide board, the name of the shop painted on in block letters. I met the printers as they were coming in to work.

"Looks as if you bore the brunt of an attack," I said.

"More than one," the printer said while unlocking the door.

"Thank goodness it looks as if Hitler's turned his attention to Russia," I said.

The assistant, an older man, looked around at the destruction and said, "Amen to that."

"I need to make two changes to *The Stage,*" I told them.

"Which pages? We can start setting the rest while you

rewrite your changes," the lead printer said.

The "Chit Chat" column was mine, handed over by Si, although he gave me a great number of hints on what the content should be. I saw a way to take care of both problems with one notice. "Just page four." I got to work on the column immediately.

When I finished, I had removed a short piece that Si suggested on a revue that was completing its run. In its place I put:

Wanda Thomas of *Have You Seen My Mother-in-Law?* broke her leg in a stage accident. She is currently convalescing in the St. Charles Central London Hospital. An open call has gone out for an actress who can sing and dance and is a quick study to replace her in the role of "Betty." The play, after touring for a year, will now open at the Regent Theatre next Tuesday instead of tomorrow.

"Does this work so that you can put out the newspaper on time?" I asked.

The printer looked over my copy. "Broke her leg?"

"Yes, I checked with the hospital. I obtained the rest from the play's producer."

"That's something you don't see very often. Most accidents that appear in *The Stage* are fatal, and that's a rarity if there hasn't been a bombing run. Otherwise, the actors drag themselves across the stage rather than admit they're injured. If they have to drop out of a play, they don't get paid."

Something, a suspicion perhaps, made me ask, "What if it was deliberate?"

"That would be really odd. The acting profession seems to be a closed group. Sort of the same as a family. They fight among themselves, but they still protect each other against outsiders. I've been reading your paper for years while setting the type. I've learned a lot about how theaters work, and they stick with their own."

"What about the stagehands? The musicians?"

The printer gave me a sideways look. "Each little group fights all the others, but if you attack the theater, they all band together. If that accident was deliberate, it wasn't anyone in the theater."

I walked from the printer's shop to our offices in Bush House. Everywhere were the signs of rebirth or at least cleanup. It was warm and sunny, and people were busy sweeping or moving rubble with an occasional major repair job. With all the trench bomb shelters in the parks that needed maintenance, there was no one to plant flowers. Volunteers were growing vegetables in the parks, though, and allotments were springing up on some private land.

I'd have preferred flowers. And peace.

It would take a long time to rebuild, but now with Germany focusing all her attention on invading Russia, we suspected Hitler wouldn't be attacking us any time soon. And that gave us time to rebuild our cities and our army, less afraid of a German invasion with every day that passed.

Si came in while I was taking off my hat and gloves. He fought with the window in my part of the office, finally wrestling it up an inch or two. Then he went into his office without saying "Good morning" and I heard him grunting and banging on the window frame there with his fist.

Our not speaking to each other was ridiculous, especially over some play director. I stuck my head in his doorway. "Good morning. Thank you for raising my window. Shall I try to help you with yours?"

After one more bang on the window frame, he said, "Try pulling up on that side while I work on this side."

We raised the window by an inch.

"Thank you," Si said. "I shouldn't have taken out my anger at Marshall Lowe on you yesterday. I apologize."

"I accept. I checked on this week's issue this morning. It's all set to go," I told him.

He nodded. "Have you heard how that actress is?"

"I called the hospital. They've set her broken leg now and she's in traction."

"Go over there. Talk to her. Find out if the theater or the Actors' Benevolent Fund or British Equity is helping with her hospital bills. And find out what happened."

"Do you want me to talk to the local police?"

"No, I'll do that. I think Marshall Lowe's days of ruining people's lives may soon be over."

Chapter Five

At the end of the day, I went to St. Charles Central London Hospital and asked for the women's orthopedic ward. I was given directions and soon found myself in a ward for six. The matron pointed out a pale young woman in the second bed on the left with her leg in plaster. "Ten minutes. She needs to build her strength up. And visiting hours will soon be over."

I walked over. "Wanda Thomas?"

She looked up at me with big, blue eyes. Her face was narrow, her bone structure delicate, and the cast on her leg in a large traction apparatus appeared to be as big as she was. "Yes?"

"I'm Olivia Redmond from *The Stage* newspaper. There's a note in the current issue about your accident. I hope you don't mind."

"No, but I'm sure it was next to a notice looking for my replacement."

I looked down, embarrassed, and then nodded. "Yes."

After a moment, Wanda pulled herself together, gave me a bright smile, and said, "That's an actor's life for you. A success one day, a disaster the next. What can I say?"

This was one of the best performances I had ever seen.

"Is British Equity or the Actors' Benevolent Fund helping with your hospital bills?"

"The Benevolent Fund is helping by paying my rent at my boarding house so I won't be kicked out and a little toward the hospital bills."

"And the Regent Theatre?"

"What about it?"

"Surely, they should be paying for part of your hospital bills at the very least." Nothing else would be fair, although there was nothing fair about any of what had happened, or indeed had happened to London in the last year.

"I've not heard from them, nor do I expect to."

"What happened that caused your leg to break?"

"'Caused' my leg to break? What a strange thing to say."

I gave her a sharp look. "Was it an accident?" I asked directly.

"What else could it have been?"

"Sabotage."

"You sound as if you are something in a Girl Guides paper. Find the Nazi saboteur hiding in the woods." She frowned. "Don't be daft."

"So, it was the first time you'd danced on the rug on that stage."

She shook her head slightly against the pillows. Her face was whiter than the pillow cover. "No. We tried it out that morning."

"And presumably nothing was wrong then, so what

changed between the morning and afternoon rehearsals?" I wasn't going to let her off until she told me the truth. If the theater made a mistake, they should pay for her hospital care.

She grabbed my hand in a surprisingly hard grip. "Don't print that. I want to be able to work again."

"What are you talking about?"

"If you make enemies for me, I'll never get another stage job in London."

"But if someone did something to harm you..."

"They can do a lot more to harm me. I want to continue to work on the London stage long after my leg heals. Don't tell anyone what I told..." Wanda fell silent as the matron bustled in.

"Time is up. This young lady needs to get her rest."

Wanda let go of my wrist and stared at me with begging eyes. I rose and headed for the door to the ward. When I turned back, she caught my eye and mouthed, *Don't tell*.

* * *

I did what she asked and didn't tell anyone, including Si. I reviewed *The Taming of the Shrew* that week as it was played outdoors on the south bank of the Thames. I hadn't seen an Elizabethan stage before, but Si assured me what they set up in Southwark Park was the real thing including the groundlings, plus the addition of modern-day amplifiers for those listening out on the street.

The stage was built in Southwark Park and the play was performed under clear skies. Every frayed costume, every warped board could be seen by the audience, but the actors performed Shakespeare's words with such assurance that we quickly forgot all the tatters, all the trees giving partial shade, and followed the play with single-minded devotion. Even those standing in the pit below the stage paid rapt attention despite the heat and humidity building that day.

I wrote notes on my program to turn into a review later. To hold everyone's attention under these conditions deserved a terrific review.

I didn't want to go back to the Regent Theatre, that night or any time. I was afraid I'd slip and point out to someone that they should pay for Wanda's hospital charges since the stage had been fine that morning. Who was she so afraid of that she wouldn't speak out?

My plans were to go to the New Theatre on Saturday night to write up a review of the Sadler's Wells Opera Company, but curiosity sent me to the Regent in the afternoon to see how things were progressing in finding a new actress to play Betty. Entering the stage door, which was once again unlocked and unguarded, I walked to the wings of the stage.

Marnie was on stage playing the mother-in-law of the play's title with two men I vaguely remembered, and generally making it obvious that the play was about her. I stood quietly, letting the jokes and the innuendo and the sound of rich theater voices flow over me.

A tap on my shoulder caused me to spin around. Old Nick said in a low voice, "Thought you'd sneak in, did you?"

"I looked for you when I came in. Who's taken Wanda Thomas's place?"

"A young bottle blonde with quite a resume in variety. What's it to you?"

"I write for *The Stage*, remember?" I said softly.

Suddenly, a bang that sounded identical to a shot went off and a section of the stage went darker than the rest. One of the men dove for cover behind the sofa as shards of glass showered the front of the stage. Marnie made a couple of half-skips out of the way without appearing to react to the noise.

Old Nick glanced around the stage and sauntered off, leaving me on my own.

"Would it be asking too much for one rehearsal to go according to plan?" the director bellowed. Marshall Lowe's request seemed aimed at the Almighty. He would certainly be able to hear him.

"That shouldn't have happened," a burly man in worn trousers, collarless shirt, and an unbuttoned waistcoat said as he began to climb up the ladder to the spotlights.

"You're right it shouldn't have happened. Fix it so we can get on with rehearsals." The director smacked his rolled-up script against his leg as he stepped out on stage, his bright red mug in his other hand.

Another man dressed the same as the first put something in a basket and readied it to go up on the hoist.

"Can't change it yet. Too hot," the man who had climbed the ladder called down.

"I'll turn off the whole bar," the man on the ground replied as he walked off toward the backstage area.

"You can't do that. We have a rehearsal to run through. And somebody sweep up this glass," the director added as a crunch was heard under his shoe.

"Sweep it up yourself," the young man who'd been in the fight the last time I'd been here told him. He was still thin and wearing an oversized suit, but now one of his eyes sported a purple bruise and sometime in the last day or two he'd been shaved. I remembered his name was Philip Bernard, the playwright.

I walked over to him. "Mr. Bernard, I'm Livvy Redmond from *The Stage*. May I talk to you about your play for our newspaper?"

All the spotlights suddenly went dark with a clank.

Bernard glanced at me and then walked toward the director.

Marshall Lowe ignored Bernard as the electrician on the ground spoke to the director. "You'll have to rehearse without the spots until we can get it repaired." Without waiting for a reply, the electrician called up, "Can you unbolt it and send it down in the basket?"

"Not yet. It needs another pair of hands up here," the man on the ladder shouted down.

"Let me empty the basket and you can pull it up while I come up." The electrician on the stage level took whatever he'd put in the basket and walked off with it. Meanwhile, the basket began its ascent.

"You're supposed to keep the lights on," the director shouted.

"Can't do that if we're going to switch out one of a row of spots," the man above said.

"Then be more careful."

"Not my fault."

The director then turned on the playwright. "Are you behind this? I swear, if you're behind these 'accidents,' I will have you arrested."

"How can I be? I just got here. It looks as if you have bigger problems than me." The young man sneered, his face dangerously close to the director's.

Lowe walked away to move into the path of the electrician crossing the stage area. "We need to put on a play without any more distractions."

The electrician shouted at the director, "It wasn't us. It's sabotage. Lock up your precious theater," at the same time, their voices growing louder as they faced each other over five feet of space.

Nelson, the producer, hurried up to the stage from the back of the auditorium saying, "What is the problem?"

They told him at the same time, trying to talk over each other.

The producer must have been used to this type of confrontation. "Fix the light," he said to the electrician, "and then bring me evidence if you think someone's playing tricks. Marshall, everyone should be able to rehearse this play in the dark, they've done it enough. And you're only missing the spots. Continue."

"We're rehearsing to get a feel for this particular theater, its dimensions and sound, and yes, the lighting. We can't do that if the lighting doesn't work," Lowe argued.

"At the moment, we're in the hands of the electricians. Surely, you can find something to do until they fix the problem."

"Ian…"

"Do what you can, Marshall."

"Did you get my message?" the director asked the producer's back.

"Yes." Nelson turned around and walked up to Lowe where he took a piece of yellow paper and tore it into little pieces. "Not another cent, Lowe."

"You can't do that."

"I just did."

That was all it took for a fight to begin. The two men appeared to be the same age, but Nelson outweighed Lowe by two stone. I hoped Nelson didn't land any punches; Lowe was too good-looking. Fortunately, the stagehands broke it up before any blood was shed.

Once they were pulled apart, Nelson adjusted his jacket, glanced at the young playwright, Philip Bernard, and walked off.

Marnie appeared at my side. "A play that starts out this badly never goes right."

"That sounds as if it was a superstition," I told her. "Isn't the theater full of sayings such as that?"

"We should have stayed in the regional theaters. We didn't have these problems there."

"I thought all actors want to appear on the West End stage."

"They do, but not when everything is going wrong." Marnie looked at the stage and shuddered.

I lowered my voice. "I heard the electrician say it was sabotage. Is that possible?" Wanda Thomas had hinted at it too.

"It was only a matter of time with Lowe directing." Marnie glared in the director's direction.

"Why?" Marshall Lowe seemed as if he was a detestable person, but still…

"That man collects enemies the same way other people collect ashtrays."

"How? Why does anyone agree to work with him if he's that difficult?" I looked at Marnie, who shook her head.

"Spend any time around here, and you'll see what I mean. Be sure to stay on Old Nick's good side. Stage doormen know everyone's secrets and can be very useful," she said before she walked back onto the stage area where her fellow performers were standing.

"Good. Vic Graybell, glad to see you found your way up from the floor," Marshall Lowe said to the man who dove behind the sofa when the spotlight exploded. He said it with a smirk and a taunting tone that could be heard throughout the backstage. "Now, if you can remain vertical for the rest of the scene, we'd all appreciate your presence."

The actor he was talking to turned beet red and was standing with slumped shoulders. He was pressing his hands into his thighs, but I could see his hands were shaking. I'd have been embarrassed if I reacted that way, but was the actor angry enough to strike out against the play to get back at the director? Would he be able to do any damage with hands that shook that way? I wondered if that was what Marnie meant by collecting enemies.

Lowe certainly wasn't trying to win a friend in Vic Graybell by making fun of him.

The producer, Ian Nelson, came up to me and gestured for me to follow him. I did and found myself in the dressing room area. Nelson stopped in the hallway and after looking around to make sure we were alone, said, "Whatever you wrote in the advertisement for a replacement for Wanda worked. We found someone who is more than Wanda's caliber willing to work for the same wages."

I stared at Nelson as if I were looking at a snake. "And you can't afford to pay any more?" I murmured.

He hesitated and then nodded.

"If she breaks a leg, will you cover her hospital bills?"

"Of course not. Actors, musicians, they are all only working for a short time and then the show closes down and they move on. They have to look out for their own health."

"Wanda had been with you for months as you played towns all over the country. Hardly a short time."

"We could have closed at any time. She was free to leave the show at any time. Acting is a precarious job. Actors and dancers, especially of Wanda's caliber," he made a face, "are out of work as much as they are in. Perhaps more. Don't worry about her. She knows what can happen, and I'm sure she's put a bit away. And anyway, that's what the Benevolent Society is for."

I shook my head and walked off, feeling disgusted and soiled from speaking with Nelson, who hurried off in the other direction.

A look around the backstage area revealed the playwright had disappeared. I'd missed a chance to talk to him and perhaps learn where the inequities of his situation rested.

Lost in my thoughts about how unfair things were, I nearly walked into the two electricians.

The younger of the two, who'd gone up the ladder first, said, "Excuse me." Then he continued with what he was saying to the older man, "It looks as if it's worth nothing but to sell it for scrap."

"Excuse me." I stepped back when I realized he was carrying a heavy metal contraption about two feet long and several inches across.

"It's a good thing we have a few stashed away. Otherwise, the war would make it impossible to replace it," the older man said.

"Excuse me. What happened to the light?"

"Fried. It's done for," the younger man said.

"'Tis the ghost," the older man said.

"Ghost? What ghost?"

"Every theater has at least one," the younger electrician said as he walked away. "We have two. One that's young and pretty and walks through walls."

The older man followed him, finishing with, "The other is malevolent. Steals things. Breaks things. Supposedly killed an actor in the last century."

I hurried after them to a cluttered storage room with everything in it, from spotlights to chair parts for the auditorium, from rope to castoff furniture to electrical wiring. "Why do you think the light was sabotaged?"

"See here?" The older man said, pointing to the base of the light bulb. Wearing thick leather gloves, he reached in to wiggle it, showing how loose it was. "That's bound to blow on you. The power arcs between the bulb and the fitting, heating it up and making the bulb blow. No electrician would make a mistake such as that. And no one but an electrician should be handling these lights."

"Did you see anyone up there with the spotlights who wasn't an electrician?" There seemed to be a story here at the Regent Theatre and I wanted to break the news.

"All the time when we're setting up a new play. Those ladders and walkways are used by everyone to hang the scenery flats so they can be raised and lowered, wiring the speakers for the special effects, as well as our work."

"So, anyone could be sabotaging the play at any time, and no one would have noticed an extra person climbing around up there." I shook my head. Someone had been careless or someone was causing trouble, and they were doing this damage right under everyone's noses.

"Probably that crazy playwright. He's really angry with Lowe," the younger man said.

"Unless it was the ghost," the older man suggested.

Chapter Six

"Don't be daft, man. No such thing as ghosts." The younger electrician set the damaged light down and walked past us out of the storage room. "It's time for some tea."

The older man gave me a weak smile. "Better than being in here with the dust and the ghosts." He gestured me out of the storage room. We both exited before he turned around and locked the door. He walked off, following the other man toward the stage door leading outside.

"Wait," I called after them. "Why are you going out to tea? There's an electric kettle sitting on that bench with all those tea mugs."

"Can't use it," the younger man said, pointing to himself and his colleague. "Not actors."

"Is it always that way in the theater?" I asked, catching up to them.

"No. Depends on the producer and director. Marshall Lowe has this quirk, he doesn't care for the riffraff socializing with the high and mighty actors on tea breaks. Nelson disagrees, but he mustn't have found this battle winnable." The younger man wiggled his fingers at me and strode outside, followed by his partner.

I decided to stroll around offstage and act as if I were watching the play while I tried to see how anyone could be causing trouble in the theater. There didn't seem to be anyone around but a young costumer with big, dark eyes who was sitting on an old couch offstage sewing with quick short stitches. I noticed that this was the brightest spot in the backstage area due to the way the stage lights shone.

"When are they going to fix the light?" the director boomed. I looked around, but I didn't see anyone except the actors on stage, the costumer, and myself.

"Tea" didn't sound as if it was a safe response. Not when the director was looking at me with murder in his eye. "Something about bulbs," I replied.

"We'll just have to work around it the same way we've have to do everything in this play. Marnie, take it from the top of the second scene."

Marnie rose from the sofa and crossed down and to the other side before she started to recite her lines. Meanwhile, a wiry, scruffy-looking man swept up the glass shards into a dust pan.

It took me a minute to recognize him. Old Nick, the stage doorman. I'd never seen him do anything before.

I moved behind the curtain currently hanging behind the set and found myself with a young lady I hadn't seen before. "Livvy Redmond from *The Stage*." I held out a hand.

She stopped rubbing at her face and reached out to shake my hand. "I'm Gloria Snelling. I play the first daughter."

"What's bothering your face? It looks a little blotchy."

She gave me a look that said I'd been less than tactful. "I've started a new brand of makeup, and it's making me itch something terrible since I put it on. If you'll excuse me, I'm going to cream it off and throw this out."

"Could I have it, please? Strange things are happening here, and this might be another one in a series."

"Come on. It's in the dressing room. And you are welcome to have it. I'll just have to throw it out. Although we just got to London with the play. Why would anyone want to attack me of all people?" Her expression was one of complete innocence. With her light brown hair done up in a scarf and wide, blue eyes, she appeared to have practiced the innocent look frequently.

"Would anyone know that makeup is specifically yours?"

"Any of the female cast or the costumers." She shook her head. "No one else would. No one else would know which dressing table is which." Then she stopped and considered. "We haven't been here long. Perhaps not even the costumers would know."

"Then this doesn't appear to be aimed at anyone. It's just another terrible prank." I didn't know why I felt so uneasy about good luck charms vanishing, lights burning out, and makeup causing rashes. Then I remembered Wanda's pale face in the hospital, because of a lack of, or missing, floor tacks.

We went into the women's dressing room. The room was no larger than Marnie's, but had to house three actresses and any costumers helping the trio get on and off the stage at their various times.

Gloria went straight to a dressing table that appeared no different than any of the others and started putting face cream on her skin before she even sat on the stool in front of it. She wiped the cream off and studied her reflection in the mirror. "Look at that. Welts. I can't go on looking this way. Pranks? Not at all. This is vicious."

I glanced through a rack of costumes, but I didn't see anything dangerous in them. "It is a nasty trick. How long did you have the makeup on?"

"Just a few minutes."

"Why don't you try to put on a layer of face cream and leave it on for a little while and see if that helps. Meanwhile, I'll take the face paint."

She picked up the pot. "And do what with it?"

"Try to get it analyzed."

"How would you get it analyzed?" She appeared more suspicious when I mentioned "analyzed."

"The newspaper I usually work for, the *Daily Premier*, uses a nearby chemist whenever they want to get something analyzed. I've been sent there with samples once or twice before. No one will think anything of it if I take this to them." I didn't tell her it was samples that other reporters had taken and the cases were usually poisonings.

"And you'll tell me the results? It is mine."

"Yes, of course. In the meantime, keep an eye on your things." *And lock the barn door after the horse escapes*, I should have added.

She nodded, her attention on her face and the soothing cream she was spreading on her skin. I slipped the small pot into my bag and went back out to watch the rehearsal from backstage.

Two young people, a man and a woman, were having a whispered argument with sweeping hand gestures. He clearly played a type, the fair-haired fellow who once saved the empire, while she played an auburn-haired best friend type. When they saw me, they stepped around a curtain and some scenery, thereby blocking my view of them.

Neither looked familiar, but I'd met less than half the cast and no one from behind the scenes except the electricians, who had just returned from their tea.

They climbed up onto the walkway high above our heads.

"This one is loose, too," the younger man said, examining one of the spots high in the air.

"So's this one. And this. Sabotage, definitely. They all could have blown," the older man said. "Who's been up here?"

So far, there had only been small tricks played. Loosening light bulbs. Taking good luck charms. Removing tacks from a rug. Slicing costumes. Adding something to face paint. Nothing much when considered individually.

Taken together, this felt as if it were a campaign against this play and this theater. One that could soon turn dangerous.

I gave up trying to figure out all the drama and tricks in

this theater and went off to see the Sadler's Wells Opera.

Chapter Seven

I arrived at my father's home just as the blackout started, having hurried from the Ealing tube station. My speed was due more from not wanting to try to find my way in the dark and less from a desire to spend time with my father.

When I unlocked the door and stepped inside, I heard men's voices at a distance, probably coming from the kitchen. I hurried down the hall, because one of the voices sounded the same as…

Adam! I shoved open the kitchen door as Adam sprang up from a chair and took me in his arms. There was nothing after that but Adam and me and our joy at being home together after a month of being separated by war. In those moments when our lips parted, I asked how long he'd known he'd get leave and he said he wanted to surprise me and he'd missed me.

He felt thinner, but I was certain I was too. I blamed it on the rationing. Adam said how he'd thought about me every day and how he'd begged for leave. I said how much I missed him. All day, every day. He asked if I still missed things I'd lost in the bombing of our flat and I said not as much as I missed him.

My father, who'd been sitting there without comment, said then that they'd eaten since I was so late with my assignment, but they'd saved me some dinner. Then he said how glad he was to have Adam visiting, even if it was only for a few days, and left the kitchen.

I didn't miss my father.

Adam picked up his crutches where they'd fallen to the floor without our noticing. I eventually ate my dinner, sharing some of it with him. He had brought some real coffee with him—I didn't ask how he'd obtained it—and we had the last two cups in the pot.

"We haven't had a proper chat since you were home in late May. How are you doing on your assignment? Can you get around well enough, or is it too much?" I asked. We were huddled close to each other at the large, wooden kitchen table. I leaned forward, afraid to take my eyes off him in case he disappeared.

"Now that it's warmer where I'm stationed, I'm finding it easier to get around. We've found a couple of ways to cut down on my walking without sacrificing what I'm there to do, so it's good." He took my hand. "I've been thinking about what you said the last time I was here, and I'm willing if you are. You're the one who will have to do all the work. I won't be around to help."

I pressed his hand in return. The idea of a baby gave me hope. "This is my father's house. He won't be too pleased. And there's such a shortage of housing now after the Blitz that we can't get another flat."

"Do you have a backup plan?"

"Any chance of getting accommodation somewhere near you?" I hoped that situation had improved.

Adam shook his head. "We're in a big manor house fifteen or twenty miles from the closest village, and there's no spare housing either place. There's spare land the MOD could build married officer quarters on, but they won't. They need the manpower and money for the war effort. Even if you were in the closest village, I couldn't get to see you any more than I do now, and you wouldn't know a soul there. What about joining Esther or Abby?"

"That would mean giving up work."

"For a while, at least, I think you'd be so busy you wouldn't notice."

"It would certainly be more restful while I try to learn to be a mother." Just visiting Esther for a weekend had been a holiday.

"Otherwise, you'd need to find help, and your father probably wouldn't appreciate another person in his house."

The loss of the flat on what we now hoped was the last day of the Blitz had been a terrible shock. May tenth had been burned into my brain forever. Fortunately, I had been visiting Abby and Sir John Summersby that weekend, and hadn't been trapped in the shelter. I had survived, unlike some of my neighbors. I just lost all my worldly goods not stored at my father's, as well as my last link to my first husband, Reggie, and a great deal of my freedom.

I'd had no other choice than to move back home with my

father. We tolerated each other at the best of times. What was that saying, "Familiarity breeds contempt"?

My father liked Adam and he was always welcome to visit, but having me move in on a permanent basis was straining his nerves. I'd been living with him in the house I'd grown up in for two months and already there were signs this would become lethal.

"Now that Hitler has invaded Russia, the war is beginning to tip in our direction. And even if we start on our first child tonight, it's another nine months before Junior is going to demand your time. Just promise me you won't work for Sir Malcolm anymore," Adam said.

"Gladly. I haven't heard from him since before we lost the flat. Maybe he can't find me." I looked at Adam with hope in my eyes.

"No. If he wanted to find you, he would. Promise me you'll turn down any assignments from Sir Malcolm from now on."

His expression was so serious I had to ask, "Why? What's going on, Adam?"

"I can't tell you. Just trust me on this."

I nodded. I wanted to know what he was talking about, but I trusted him and I knew there were secrets, knowledge from the army, that he couldn't share with me.

* * *

The next morning was Sunday. We stayed in bed late and barely dressed in time for church. My father gave me a look that resembled a storm cloud and then greeted Adam as a welcome guest.

After church, my father stopped to talk to a few members of the congregation that I'd known most of my life. He proudly introduced Adam, who had to answer the same questions about his crutches from everyone, over and over. Adam handled the interrogation much better than I would.

I was completely ignored.

Once we left the churchyard, we walked to the Underground station and rode the train into the West End to my father's favorite hotel for Sunday dinner. I'd gone there with him a few times since the Blitz began, but this was first time Adam had been inside the dining room in ages.

Beside wear and tear, the room had suffered damage at one end where two windows had been blown out and fire had scorched the carpeting beneath them during an attack in the latter stages of the Blitz. There was a tiny stain on our tablecloth and a chip on the edge of one of the plates. The food wasn't up to its earlier standards, either. Portions were smaller and the coffee was the same wretched ground weeds we had at home.

One thing hadn't changed. The wine list was nearly as robust as before.

After dinner, we went for a walk, ending up by Westminster Abbey and the Houses of Parliament. "It's good to remind myself they're still there," Adam said quietly.

I looked around at the groups surrounding us. Many of them were in uniform the same as Adam. Were they all there for the same reason, for a reminder, or were there so many in our country who'd never traveled to London before?

Due to bombing damage, our ride through the Underground was twice interrupted by switching tracks before we finally returned to my father's area, and once we'd returned to the house, Adam proclaimed himself tired. My father insisted I stay with him and heat up some soup left by Mrs. Johnson, his housekeeper.

Not wanting to aggravate my father any more than I usually did, I started to heat the soup, summer vegetables with a slight taste of meat broth. Adam then decided he was hungry and joined us in the kitchen.

The two men in my life got into a discussion about when the United States might enter the war. That moved on to who was going to win in Russia, Hitler or Stalin?

We finished the soup, I did the dishes, and still my father wanted to talk to Adam about the war even though my husband's eyes were drooping. Then it hit me. Either my father wanted assurance from Adam that we were going to win, or he wanted someone to talk to who wasn't me.

Bringing a baby into this house might be an unfortunate choice.

Chapter Eight

Adam and I had one more day of warm, sunny weather to spend together and we made the most of it, sleeping late, sitting in my father's back garden, staying out of Mrs. Johnson's way, and taking the Underground to the site of our bombed-out building. I hadn't been by since shortly after the destruction when Adam was last in town, and I was surprised at how much of the rubble had been cleared away.

Adam was again shocked at how completely the building had been destroyed, and said he was thankful I hadn't been home that weekend. He gladly accepted my offer of lunch at a soup bar. "Think they'll ever rebuild our building?"

I shrugged. "Maybe after the war." They'd have to start from the cellar up.

When we returned to my father's house, Mrs. Johnson was gone and my father hadn't yet come home. We reveled in the privacy up in our room and then in the back garden.

When my father returned, all he said was "Adam, what do you think of this?" or "Adam, should I try that?" He never asked for *my* opinion on anything.

When I'd had quite enough of being ignored, I gave him my opinion anyway. I don't know why I bothered. My father never considered my opinion.

The next day, Tuesday, Adam had to begin his slow, mind- and body-numbing trek back north on our increasingly aging railway. I went with him to the train station where we said our goodbyes and gave each other the last words of love we'd hear from each other's lips for some time, until Adam got leave to visit London again.

I stood on the platform, watching his train slowly roll out of the station, and then headed on foot to Bush House to the offices of *The Stage*.

When I walked in the door, Si said, "I hear you've been investigating all the shenanigans going on at the Regent."

"You know about Wanda Thomas and her broken leg because someone took the tacks out of the rug. Another actress, Gloria Snelling, had something added to her stage makeup. At least I think she had. I need to take it down to the pharmacy to have it analyzed."

"She kept the skin cream on her face for a day and by now her face is completely healed up. In time for opening night," Si told me.

"Anything happen in the last couple of days?" I asked.

"Arguments. Nerves. You'd better take that face cream to the pharmacy if you're going to have it checked out. Then I want you to go back to the Regent, see what's going on. See if that playwright has been back to fight with Lowe again."

"Was there trouble while I was off?"

"Yes. Bernard started another fight yesterday with Lowe. This time, Lowe called the police. Bernard's been permanently barred from the Regent, at least while Lowe is there. And Lowe said that despite buying Bernard's play, he isn't obligated to stage it. He'll just think of the money he paid Bernard over the weekend as a loss."

"He just paid him this past weekend? I thought he bought the play a year ago."

"He paid for an option a year ago. This past weekend, he approved the rewrites and paid a fortune, in cash, for the play."

"Why?" I said frowning. "One day he pays a fortune in cash for the play and the next day bans Bernard from the theater?"

"I think he was just trying to get Bernard's attention. Let him know who is boss. It succeeded. The police had to escort Bernard out of the theater."

"Are all plays and theaters as plagued with bad luck and fights as this one?" I was glad I never went in for a stage career.

"This one started badly, long before the cast brought it to London. Just rumor, you understand."

"Si. Tell me what you know." I made my tone as unyielding as I could.

He held up his hands. "All right. All right. Philip Bernard claims to have originally written the play about his family. The real story, I've been told, involves a murder and was quite a tragedy. The wrong person was hanged, as they discovered too late."

"How awful." That must be the nightmare every

constable and judge in our nation carried to their beds on sleepless nights.

"Bernard was put into care. A misery he never got over."

"But that's not the plot now." I'd seen parts of the play. It was a comedy.

"Marshall Lowe saw something in the play and bought an option on it. He then made it into a comedy, or used a totally separate play, with the mother figure, Marnie's role, disappearing and reappearing as part of the plot. She's the star of the show, but in Bernard's original play, she was the killer."

"Good grief. I don't blame the playwright for being furious. It was his life story, in a way. If Lowe really did use his play." Actors were notoriously thin-skinned. I wondered if playwrights were, too.

"Bernard and Lowe fought, but Lowe had him tied up in contracts. Lowe claimed no one can put on a tragedy in wartime. He would stage it after the war, but Bernard said the man had already taken his life story and made a travesty of it. Before they took the play starring Marnie on the road, Lowe asked for rewrites in Bernard's play from him before he'd pay for it. Assured Bernard he'd put it on after they returned to London. After the war."

"So, when the play went out on tour, Lowe and Bernard had a deal. A deal they didn't understand in the same way? And since they returned, the play's been plagued with nasty tricks?"

"Yes, just since it's come to London. Everything was fine

when the play was out on tour."

I considered the possibilities. "Is Bernard pulling these tricks or is a family member or friend of Bernard doing this?"

"Not that anyone can prove in either case. Philip Bernard is a loner after spending years in care. He didn't have a family after they were all killed, one way or another, as far as I know. There are rumors the boy was tortured by his grandmother before he was placed in care."

"I can't see Marnie playing a role in a play such as that. She's known as a comedienne." I couldn't remember her acting in a tragedy, not even Shakespeare.

"She's spent her career building up her reputation in comedy. She wouldn't throw it away on a story as depressing as this with no happy ending for anyone," Si told me. "From what I understand about the two plays from Lowe, except for them both being about families run by the mother-in-law, there's not much in common. Lowe swears he didn't create the comedy from the tragedy."

"What does Bernard say?"

"It's a direct copy, turned into a comedy."

"So, the nasty tricks could be Bernard getting even with what he sees as Lowe mocking him," I said. "Why, with all this fighting between the two, did Bernard sell his play to Lowe?"

"I've heard that Bernard said Lowe was the best director he knows of and that he understands tragedy."

"Where does Bernard live? I might try to interview him for *The Stage*."

"We wouldn't run it," Si warned me.

"That's all right. It's just an excuse to talk to him and find out what he's up to."

Si shrugged and told me Bernard was living in a rooming house three doors down from the pub on the corner a street down from the Regent.

"Has any of the damage been reported to the police yet?"

Si shook his head. "Well, only that Bernard can't come back to the Regent."

"I'll take the makeup to the pharmacy to be analyzed and then I'll go watch the rehearsal at the Regent. Maybe I'll be lucky and catch someone causing trouble."

"The first performance in London will take place tonight. Six-thirty, so the audience can get home before the blackout. I want you to cover it. This afternoon, there's a new comedy in rehearsal at the Princess Alexandra Theatre. I want you to watch for a while. See how this rehearsal is different from the one at the Regent."

When I started to question him, he added, "Not for an article. I just want you to see the difference."

I nodded and left the office. The first place I went to was Fleet Street to the *Daily Premier*. I asked Sir Henry if he'd pay for an analysis and then had to explain what was occurring at the Regent.

When I finished, Sir Henry shook his head. "I want you to cover this story for me. For the *Daily Premier*. It may not end in disaster, but it certainly seems to be on that path. Before you turn in the makeup at the pharmacy on our account, write up everything that's happened so far and give it to Colinswood."

I nodded and rose to leave.

"Heard anything from Adam?"

"He was here for a couple of days. He just went back this morning."

"I thought I noted a spring in your step."

I shook my head at him and left to find a vacant desk in Colinswood's section of the newspaper building. It didn't take me long to type a list of all the events that had happened at the Regent. Then I quickly filled Mr. Colinswood in and headed for the pharmacy.

The bell over the door jingled when I walked in. I could only step in a few feet before I was stopped by the counter. A woman in a pressed, glowing white nurse's apron asked if she could help me. I explained I was there on behalf of the *Daily Premier* and needed an analysis of the contents of the small pot I pulled out of my bag.

"What is Sir Henry involved with this time?" she asked. "No, don't tell me. Poison in makeup? That's a new one." She started to write up a card to affix to the pot.

"This wasn't lethal. It just caused welts. Or a rash."

"That's still vicious. Sir Henry does keep our work interesting."

While she wrote, I looked around. Jars of all sorts and shapes filled the dark wood paneled shelves in the small front room. The counter in front of the shelves was paneled in the same wood. Big black and white tiles covered the floor. I doubted the interior had changed since Edwardian times.

"We'll try to have the results for you by Thursday."

"Thank you." I took the small paper she gave me as a receipt and walked over to the Princess Alexandra. After introducing myself to the producer and assuring him I would be back for opening night, he let me sit in on part of the rehearsal. "Did you have a tour in other towns first?" I whispered.

"The MOD requires it of any play that wants to be shown on the West End. Our duty is to entertain the troops and the factory workers first in wartime. The West End is expected to wait." The producer gave a sigh when he finished.

The play was funny and the timing was perfect. The rehearsal was more for lighting and sound checks. Everything was performed with businesslike competency.

Something I hadn't seen much of at the Regent.

I left a while later and headed off to the Regent Theatre. It had been seventy-two hours since I'd last been there, and who knew what chaos had ensued while I was enjoying my time off with Adam.

I went in the stage door as usual with no one to stop me. When I reached the backstage area, I met up with the actor playing the vicar just coming off stage. "Robbie Day, isn't it?" I asked. He'd introduced himself the first day I'd come to the Regent when I was drafted in to read Betty's part in the rehearsal.

"Yes. It's nice when someone remembers your name." He gave me a wide grin. "The director is running us through one last rehearsal to show us we can get through the play at least one time without disaster striking."

"I haven't been around the last few days. What's happened?"

"Gloria had something added to her makeup that caused a rash. That playwright chap was thrown out of the theater. And then we had the power cut backstage."

"It was only the backstage area?" I asked.

"That was the odd bit. The front of the house was fine."

"Maybe it was a blown fuse." At least, that sounded sensible to me.

"There were no blown fuses."

"Then what happened?"

"There's a couple of big switches backstage that cut power to the whole building in case of emergency. We were all out front or on stage when we heard a loud bang and everything from the stage back went dark. There was no one back there to throw the switch. And only the backstage switch was flipped off." Robbie sounded young and amazed. Looking at him from the audience, you'd think he was more than my age, perhaps in his late thirties, and that he really was a vicar, tall and thin and a bit gullible.

"Was there a lock on the switch?"

"Yes. Well, there had been a half hour earlier."

"Who has the keys?" I asked.

"One of them was on a big ring of keys kept in the front office. It was found backstage after they turned the lights back on."

"Someone sneaked in the stage door and took the lock off and threw the switch while everyone, cast and crew, was in front. After they'd already stolen the keys from the front office." That sounded to me as the most plausible explanation, which still didn't sound very plausible.

"Old Nick rarely stays at his post. I know that, but at the time we're talking about, he was in the front of the house with us and there was a bobby at the stage door wanting a word with one of the stagehands. And the bobby wasn't going to leave the exit until he questioned the man."

"Why didn't the bobby...?" Now I was confused.

"Marshall Lowe had everyone—stagehands, electricians, dressers, actors, everyone—out front where he could give them a good dressing down. He is furious about all the pranks going on and wants them stopped. Nobody was excused. Not even Marnie Keller."

"Was everybody there? Was everybody really there?" I was doubtful and I'm sure my tone showed it.

"Jobs aren't that plentiful in the theater right now, especially in London. Lowe's a swine, but his productions pay. I've been in this show since the beginning, which means I've had a paying job for nearly a year," Robbie Day told me. "All over the country, mind, but I'm single so it's no hardship. And being out of London during the Blitz was an extra bonus." He looked at me with raised eyebrows. "Do I look stupid enough to ignore an order from our great director and lose this good spot?"

"The stagehands and electricians work for the theater,

not Marshall Lowe. Why would they come when he calls?"

"Money."

I raised my eyebrows at him.

"The Regent is owned and operated by Harry Morris, yes, that Harry Morris of variety hall fame. I think Lowe has something on him."

"What could Lowe have on him? Morris's life—from his divorces and girlfriends to his drinking and brawling—his life's an open book." I'd read about it often enough in the newspapers. His life always guaranteed a juicy read.

"I don't know. Maybe he's bought the whole Lowe legend. The man is a genius of the theater, the man always makes everyone money, the man can always pick a winner. Who wouldn't want to have him putting on a production in his theater? Or maybe it's something more sinister."

"What?" I leaned forward as he lowered his voice.

"Between you and me, I think Lowe has something on Morris, going back to the days when Morris was looking at a prison sentence for something drink- or drug- fueled and Lowe came up with a rock-solid alibi for Morris at the last moment. Now, if Lowe says to hire more people, Morris does. If Lowe says to fire someone for insubordination, he does."

Robbie Day sounded bitter. I wondered for a moment if he'd been drinking, but I couldn't smell any telltale fumes.

"Have the pranks stopped now?" I asked.

"Nothing has happened since yesterday before lunch break."

"Good. Maybe it's over with."

Robbie's snort told me what he thought of my suggestion.

"What happened with the bobby?"

"He was called in when everyone saw what had caused the power cut. He swore no one had gone past him for the ten minutes he'd been waiting for the stagehand. He told them to lock the stage door and then took the stagehand away. Must have been the wrong man because the stagehand was back in a couple of hours."

"And by then Old Nick was away from the door again?"

"No. He was back saying he'd been there all the time." Robbie raised his eyebrows.

If Morris or Lowe or Nelson, the producer, didn't start locking that door or get a new stage doorman, someone was going to get killed with one of these pranks

Chapter Nine

I spoke to Ian Nelson next to find out where the reporter from *The Stage* would sit for the premier performance of *Have You Seen My Mother-in-Law*? Then I headed for the stage door where the small, shabby stage doorman sat in his rickety, cast-off stuffed chair. When he heard my footsteps, he hid a half-pint of liquor down inside the chair arm.

I ignored it and put on my charming voice. "Why do you go by 'Old Nick'?"

"What's it to you?"

"I'm Olivia Redmond from *The Stage*. How long have you worked here?"

He looked at me out of the corner of his eye. "Why?"

"I'm interviewing you for the newspaper. How long have you been here? Is this the only theater you've worked at? What did you do before you came here?"

"Whoa. Whoa. Whoa. That's too many questions, woman."

"All right. How long have you worked at your current position?" I pulled out my notebook and pencil.

"Since well before the war started. Before our current king was on the throne."

"I imagine you've met most of the stars of the West End."

He nodded. "Quite a few."

"Who's your favorite?"

"That would be telling. Besides, a man in my position can't play favorites."

"Oh, of course not," I replied. "Especially when you receive the telegrams and flowers on opening night. Who's received the most by your estimate?"

"Gracie Fields when she played here at the start of the war. Now, that woman is a star. And she's kind to everyone in the theater, including me. Sees me to the price of a pint every time she plays here."

That told me everyone in the theater community knew that Old Nick was unreliable. And that served the person pulling the wicked pranks well.

"I bet you know every nook and cranny of this building," I said.

"Better than anyone else here. Need a hidey-hole for when the bombs are dropping."

"You have your own bomb shelter here in the theater? How—amazing."

I could hear Mr. Colinswood saying, "Amazing? You have an entire language to use and you said amazing?" Mr. Colinswood, having lost most of his experienced reporters to the war effort, was now trying to turn me into a good reporter. Well, adequate.

My choice of words didn't bother Old Nick at all. "Yes.

Never know when you might need to find a safe place to wait out the present danger."

"I hope to see you tonight." I put a coin in his outstretched hand.

He gave me a salute and settled down in his ratty stuffed chair.

I went to my father's and dressed in one of my surviving evening gowns before heading back out on the Underground, escaping before my father returned home.

Half of the audience was in uniform, but then, so was half of London. This July day was clear and the sunshine was beating down on us when I queued up outside with the rest of the theatergoers. Before the war, the show would have started much later, but everything now was timed around the blackout.

I took a program and fanned myself with it as I nodded to Nelson on my way into the auditorium. It was opening night and the poor producer looked worried out of his mind. With all the pranks leading up to that moment, Nelson wasn't the only one afraid of what would happen with an audience present.

I almost wanted to settle myself in the wings and watch from there, to see if I could catch the prankster before he could act that night, but I knew it wouldn't be appreciated. I'd learned almost immediately in my new position that opening night nerves could be found in every theater in London. I settled into my seat in front of the stage and waited for the lights to dim.

I'd seen enough in rehearsals to know the plot that Marshall Lowe had put together was a simple domestic comedy, with the main character, played by Marnie Keller, disappearing and reappearing. I still didn't know if the play we'd see that night was or wasn't from the tragedy by Philip Bernard.

There were a lot of funny lines. Lowe, or whoever he stole the play from, was a gifted scriptwriter, and the cast knew how to play off one another. What wasn't explained was why everyone was always worrying about where the mother-in-law of the title was. In the Bernard story, she was a thief, an abuser, a liar, and a killer. In this, she was merely eccentric, lively, madcap.

And you never knew where she'd pop up next in the play.

The audience was quickly settling in their seats, filling the auditorium as they murmured among themselves in anticipation. Finally, the lights dimmed, and the curtain rose. The scene was a large, middle-class drawing room. I could see the rug where the dancing accident had taken place. I hoped it was well tacked down tonight.

One of the sons-in-law, played by Bud Cosby, perhaps the second best-known actor in the group, was sitting reading the newspaper when Marnie walked in and the audience erupted in applause. From then on, there were plenty of laughs as the actors ran through the lines I had heard while watching the rehearsals.

Marnie Keller, the mother-in-law, appeared three more times in the first act, leaving before the character looking for her came back on stage.

When it came time for the jive dancing, Bud Cosby and Diana Carroll, the replacement actress for Wanda Thomas, went through a spirited routine to a jazz number amid loud applause. I found I was holding my breath until it finished without a slip.

Shortly afterward, the first act ended just as Marnie Keller came back onto the empty stage.

Not wanting an overpriced drink, and finding I was curious, I worked my way backstage to find out if Old Nick was in his proper place.

He wasn't. Just then I looked over and saw him coming out of the door that led to the storage room that held cleaning supplies and who knew what else. Probably his liquor supply. "Is that your office?" I asked, striding over to him.

It took him a minute to focus on my face. "Ah, the writer woman."

"Were you sleeping in there?"

"No." He tried to walk around me, but I blocked his path.

"How long were you in there?" I could smell the booze on his breath.

"Just a couple of minutes."

I could hear the stagehands moving around the set, changing the stage now to be the back garden of the house seen in the second act. The young, dark-eyed costumer I'd seen sewing on the couch was at work there again backstage. An actress, her makeup on thick enough to be seen in the balcony, hurried in our direction but then turned off toward the dressing rooms, talking to herself.

I glanced over to the table next to Old Nick's chair. "Long enough for telegrams to pile up."

"They've been coming in since before the show started. I'll have plenty of time to sort them during the second act."

Marshall Lowe walked up to us, his silver hair wet with sweat and his mouth opening and closing. His handsome face looked slack and his bright red mug started to slip from his grasp.

"What's wrong?" I asked, moving to grab the mug and help him into Old Nick's chair.

He stumbled a step or two. "Need…air." Then he keeled over onto the floor.

"Quick, find a bobby. There must be one on this street," I told Old Nick as I knelt to loosen the director's collar and white tie. He started having convulsions and I didn't know what to do for him. I was frightened and confused. The doorman still hovered over me. I snapped at him, "Go now. Get help!"

Chapter Ten

Old Nick ran to where the stagehands were hurrying backstage. They rushed over, hovering over us and asking questions.

"You, get a bobby," I said to the youngest and fastest looking. By now I could see the director's face was flushed pink.

The young man nodded and raced outside, clearly having more sense than Old Nick.

The chief stagehand knelt across from me, trying to stop Lowe from banging his head on the floor. "What is that smell?"

I leaned forward and sniffed. "Bitter almonds."

"Good grief. How could he have taken cyanide?" the stagehand said. "And where?" We were deliberately keeping our voices down, not certain how much the audience might hear.

"There's rat poison in the cleaning supply cupboard," one of his assistants said, hurrying back toward us.

"How did you know…? Bitter almonds and rat poison?"

"Ned and me, we're first-aiders for a local ARP unit. It's part of our training, recognizing poisons, stuff such as cyanide," the chief stagehand told me, "in case the Nazis start dropping poisons on us."

"I didn't think the play was that bad," the other assistant said.

"What? You think this is suicide?" I asked, my frown showing my opinion of his joke.

"He will be a popular corpse," the chief stagehand said. He held out his hand over the shuddering victim. "Gil Baker."

I shivered before I shook his hand. "Livvy Redmond. From *The Stage*."

He saw my reluctance and said, "Not the usual place to meet someone. Sorry."

"Not your fault." I paused. "It isn't, is it?"

"I couldn't stand him, but I wouldn't do this. Not after training to help my fellow Londoners."

By now, actors and electricians were coming over to find out what was going on, muttering amongst themselves. Lowe's body had gone completely, ominously still. With a cry, the young costumer dropped her sewing and started to crumple to the floor. The middle-aged props man gathered her and her sewing up and walked her away to the sofa where I'd seen her working. "It's all right, Millie. There are no bombs falling. You're safe enough."

"The audience is getting restless. They know the interval's been too long," one of the actors said. "What do we do?"

"What we always do," Marnie said. "We know this play. All of us. Gentlemen, when we're in position, raise the curtain." She strode off, followed by Robbie Day in his vicar's collar. Two of the stagehands hurried away, and in a moment, we heard the curtain rise and the audience quiet.

The crowd around the still corpse began to drift away to do their tasks until it was only Gil Baker and me. He picked up the mug I'd set down next to me when Lowe collapsed. Sniffing it, he said, "Bitter almonds there, too. We need to show that to the police. And for pity's sake, don't let anyone drink it or spill it."

"I won't."

"I've got to get back to work. While my apprentice is out looking for a bobby, will you be all right on your own? You don't faint at the sight of corpses, do you?"

I thought of how many I'd seen since I started this job. "No."

"Nick, keep an eye out for the coppers."

"Aye."

The stagehand rose on creaking knees and patted my shoulder.

I gave him a weak smile. "The show must go on."

As Gil Baker walked off, I glanced over to see Old Nick take a swig from a half-pint of liquor as he stood in the doorway of the cleaning supply room. He didn't appear to be anyone you could count on in a crisis.

"Did he have anything to eat or drink beside the tea?" I whispered, trying not to be heard onstage.

"Just the cuppa."

"When?"

"At the end of the first act. Does that at the end of every first act in every play. Has for years." Old Nick tapped the side of his nose.

"Did you see who made his tea?"

"He did. He always did."

"Then what did he do?" I hoped Old Nick could point me toward the murderer.

"Went to tell someone their job."

That sounded so very like Marshall Lowe. "With or without his mug?"

"With. And now I have my own tasks to see to, don't I?"

I'd seen the kettle in the backstage area, with a motley collection of mugs and cups. Mugs and cups that could only belong to the actors. I'd been told the crew, employees of the theater, couldn't use the electric kettle. "Did he fix the tea himself tonight?" I asked again, testing him.

"Must have." Old Nick sounded belligerent, although I suspected he permanently didn't want to take any responsibility.

A bobby arrived with the young stagehand, and Old Nick faded off to make himself invisible. The bobby leaned over the director and nudged him, harshly whispering in his ear in an attempt to rouse him. Then he asked me, "Is he dead?"

"He collapsed there and he's not breathing," I offered. The young stagehand backed up a couple of steps and then hurried off to do his part for the play.

"Do you have a telephone I can use to call the stationhouse?" The bobby sounded uncertain. He also seemed very young.

"There's one over by the tea table."

The bobby moved next to me, still holding his helmet against his stomach, and bent over and picked up the red mug on the floor. "Whose cup is this?"

"The director's," I told him.

"And who is the dead man?"

"The director."

"Who made his tea? This is tea?"

"I was in the audience the first half," I told him. "And I don't know who made the tea, although he customarily made it himself. Please note, the tea and the body smell of bitter almonds."

The bobby began his call just as Ian Nelson came backstage with a puzzled expression on his face. "The timing this second half is off. Where's Lowe?"

I pointed at the body.

"Good grief." He walked around with his hands in his hair, making little moaning sounds. "This is dreadful. Where can I find another director on such short notice?"

I just stared at Nelson, certain it was shock that would make him say such a callous thing.

"Have we contacted the police?"

"The bobby is just phoning for reinforcements now," I told him, gesturing toward the young man.

As the bobby hung up the receiver, Nelson hurried up to him. "I'm the producer. What happened to Mr. Lowe?"

"He appears to be dead, sir."

"Why?"

If the audience hadn't heard us before, they certainly heard that one-word cry. That it was the producer who so forgot himself as to make that much noise struck me as strange.

I had remembered to keep my voice down as had Old Nick. Even the bobby had tried to whisper.

* * *

The police allowed the play to continue to its conclusion, when Marnie as the mother-in-law reappears to her entire family and tells them she was collecting the proof that they were indeed the inheritors of a castle. As the rest of the cast made "ooh" and "aah" sounds, she informed them the castle was theirs, but the Ministry of Defense had taken it over for the duration.

I listened from the wings, staying out of the way of the forensic officers, coroner, and police who were busy sealing off all the exits to the theater. A man in a clean but rumpled suit and well-polished shoes walked up next to me and asked in a deep, quiet voice when the play would end.

"This is the last scene, followed by the curtain calls," I whispered.

"I was told you found the body."

"No. I was talking to the stage doorman, Old Nick, when Mr. Lowe, still alive, walked up to us, fell down writhing, and died. Who are you?" I hoped he wasn't from a rival paper. I guessed he was about fifty, old enough to avoid being called up.

He showed me his identity card. Detective Inspector Dawson.

Chapter Eleven

An inspector and forensic officers, even a coroner, didn't have far to go from Scotland Yard to the Regent Theatre. They could have walked it, since the sun was still shining, in a few minutes. Up Whitehall and then Haymarket. Somehow, I was willing to guess that the inspector and the doctor, being in charge of the body and the crime scene, rode there in a police car.

"And you are?"

"Olivia Redmond, a reporter from *The Stage*. On loan from the *Daily Premier*."

"Please wait here until I have a chance to take your statement. And do not phone either of your papers." He walked off as the curtain call started, leaving me in no doubt that he hadn't given me a request.

The cast began to come off the stage, congratulating each other on surviving a performance under trying circumstances. And all of them were praising Bud Cosby. "Why him?" I asked Gloria Snelling as she walked toward the dressing rooms.

"He's worked as a director before, and his part is involved in most of the scenes. He stepped up and helped us to stay focused under these ghastly circumstances. Did a good job, too."

I wrote a quick reminder in my notebook and then continued watching the activity backstage, both by the cast and crew and the police. For once no one was trying to throw me out. The inspector wanted to talk to me.

It was Bud Cosby who read out the congratulatory telegrams directed to the entire cast and crew in the dressing room hallway, out of the way of the police and corpse. There was much hugging and back-slapping, and several members of the cast asked for my impressions. Since I now knew all the actors' names from the program, I could make my congratulations personal.

Almost everyone had been released by the police before Inspector Dawson and Sergeant Mullins came over to where I was waiting after I'd been directed to sit in the still steamy auditorium. Even Old Nick had slunk off. Mullins sat in the row in back of me, and Dawson took a seat one over from mine.

"Why are you filling in as a reporter for *The Stage* when you normally work for the *Daily Premier*?" Dawson began after getting my name and address.

"My boss is lending me out as a favor for a friend."

"Because you're that good?" His words sounded as if they were a challenge.

"No. I think it's because I'm expendable." I gave him a smile and a shrug.

He fought down a smile and continued. "I've been told

you've been around this theater more often than other theaters or other reporters for *The Stage*."

"Has anyone told you about all the bad luck they've had, or pranks that have been carried out, since *Have You Seen My Mother-in-Law?* arrived here from their tour?"

"Suppose you tell me."

I did.

When I finished, the inspector said, "And you have a theory as to who's behind these pranks?"

"No. Old Nick is unreliable, which is how I think most of the pranks were carried out, by someone walking in while he was away from his post. I certainly didn't expect anything along the lines of murder. Have you found any clues? Well, beside his tea mug."

The inspector looked at me as if I was to be tolerated, but only barely. "Where was the doorman when you first arrived backstage?"

"Stumbling out of the storeroom. I think that's where he keeps his liquor."

"The storeroom where the rat poison is kept."

"I didn't know that. Is that what killed him?" I reached into my bag and pulled out my notebook again, only to see the inspector shake his head at me.

"We don't know what killed him yet." He took on a more conversational tone. "You're an outsider. Do you think this troop of players is a happy bunch?"

"Neither happy nor unhappy. With all the accidents, everyone was a bit on edge, and no one liked the director.

For a group that had been together for a year, they seemed to be almost strangers to each other. Maybe the producer can explain it. I can't. Do you think an insider in this play killed him?"

The inspector turned the question back on me. "Who do you think killed Marshall Lowe?"

"I'd find out where a writer named Philip Bernard was tonight."

"Why?"

"He wrote a play that he sold to Marshall Lowe. He claims Lowe changed his tragedy into the comedy that was performed here tonight. Lowe claimed he didn't and he was saving the tragedy for after the war, since apparently you can't put on a tragedy in wartime. I've seen those two men come to blows."

"Did Lowe pay this Bernard for the play?"

"Oh, yes, I believe so, they've never argued about money. But the play is apparently based on Bernard's childhood. His grandmother killed his mother but his uncle was tried and hanged for it before anyone figured out it was the grandmother. In the meantime, the grandmother tortured him. Such a sad story."

I was released then to try to catch the last train home. As I rushed up the aisle toward the backstage area and the stage door, Inspector Dawson said, "If you remember anything else, we'll be working out of Scotland Yard."

* * *

The next morning, I headed to Philip Bernard's rooming

house before work. I wanted to interview him before the police did, to see if he was guilty of the sabotage or the murder. When the door was opened to my knock, a bleached blonde wearing bright red lipstick answered the door. "I'm here for Philip Bernard," I said.

"I'm so sorry," the woman said, sounding sincere. "Top floor in the back."

Puzzled at her response, I nodded before climbing three flights of stairs and knocking on his door. When there was no answer, I turned the knob. The door opened.

I walked in to the darkened room, immediately aware of the unwashed, rancid smell. I went to the window and pushed back the blackout curtains to get some light in.

The room was as filthy as it smelled. I dragged open the window as a woman's voice said behind me, "I'm sorry it's such a fright, but Phil wouldn't let anyone in here. Our landlady was in a right state about it, but even she couldn't get him to let her come in to change the sheets these last couple of weeks."

"Why wouldn't he?"

"He was afraid someone would steal his new play. After his experience with Marshall Lowe, I'm not surprised."

"You knew Philip well? Spoke to him often?"

"As well as anyone here. Phil was a very private man, but we all try to look after each other. In the end, he just turned his back on all of us."

The bedsheets hadn't been laundered in weeks, that was clear. There were several stacks of books, most overdue from the library. A small table held a typewriter and a few pages of the beginning of a play. I read through it quickly. The main character was a boy who'd been kept in a workhouse left over from Dickens's time. Dickens was much better.

Also, there was a wooden chair and a wardrobe. The room was plain and miserable and dreary.

I opened the wardrobe. A depressed-looking suit and shirts were hanging there, while at the bottom were trinkets that on closer look must have been the missing items taken from the Regent. On the other side was a pile of dirty clothes. There was no sign of the money for the play or the script of the play that Lowe had bought.

"I'll leave you to it. Again, I'm sorry. Phil was nice."

"It sounds as if you're friends. I'm glad." Philip Bernard was a man in need of friends.

Once she left, I went over the wardrobe carefully but still didn't find the money or the play. Same for under the thin mattress. No loose floorboards, no rug.

Wait. The woman had said that Phil *was* nice. Had they already arrested him?

There was nothing to see except the trinkets, and I didn't have the heart to take them back to the theater. I left everything as I found it, shutting the window, and closed the door behind me, afraid the police would be there any moment.

The house was silent and I didn't want to run into the police or Philip Bernard immediately after going through his things. I was sure the guilt on my face would give me away.

There was no one on the stairs or in the front hall when I left, so I escaped without being seen.

At least I hadn't found any rat poison there.

Next, I went to *The Stage* office, wrote up a report on the murder of Marshall Lowe, and then telephoned it in to Mr. Colinswood. I was halfway through my review of the play when Si arrived, looking wilted already in the morning heat. Still, his yellow waistcoat was lively.

I could tell when he reached the article on the murder I'd left on his desk by the curse followed by a shout of my name.

I walked to the doorway to his office and looked at him, eyebrows raised.

"So, someone finally killed the…no, you don't need to hear what he was."

"You didn't care for him, did you, Si?"

"No, I did not, but that was between him and me." He scowled up at me. "The police don't know who did it? And not even certain about the murder weapon? Maybe it was his evil nature killing him by natural causes."

"Most likely rat poison kept in the theater, but the inspector wasn't committing himself until he gets the autopsy report."

"But they think it was someone in his current play."

"With Old Nick on the stage door? You've heard of Old Nick? It could have been anyone in London."

For some reason, my statement upset Si. His eyes widened and his hand shook when he reached for a pencil. The top of his head was bathed in sweat. "Have you given this story to the *Daily Premier?* This is more their line than ours. I need your review, and leave the drama out."

"You shall have it shortly." I went back to my desk and finished the review, naming all the principal players and lavishing praise. They certainly deserved it. They'd done the second half under dreadful circumstances.

I turned in the review and was choosing which play to review the coming weekend when there was a knock on the door. I looked up to see Inspector Dawson and Sergeant Mullins enter the office.

"Simon Chapell?"

I nodded toward the inner office, where I heard Si banging on his typewriter. They walked over and shoved the partly open door out of their way.

"Simon Chapell?"

"Yes?"

"We want you to accompany us to Scotland Yard to answer some questions."

"What? Why?"

The policemen were facing into Si's office and didn't see me spring to my feet. "Is this concerning the death of Marshall Lowe?"

"Yes," the inspector answered, sounding annoyed, and not looking in my direction.

"Well, Si couldn't have done it. He's not been down to the Regent Theatre," I said. There were plenty of people ahead of him with better motive and opportunity.

"Is that what he told you?"

"No, that's what I know. I cover the plays and he reports on the variety shows and takes care of the ads. I've not seen him at the Regent once."

"Ah...that's not quite accurate," Si said.

"Si, what's going on?" I heard the hesitation in my voice.

"I didn't kill him, Livvy. I didn't do any of those pranks."

"Simon Chapell, you are to come with us and help us with our enquiries regarding the death of Marshall Lowe," the inspector said.

"No," Si moaned.

"Just come with us, sir," the sergeant said, sounding determined and a little frightening.

"But what about Philip Bernard? He publicly threatened Marshall Lowe." I crossed my arms and planted my feet to block their way. I couldn't tell them I'd just found the missing trinkets from the Regent in his room.

"Mrs. Redmond, Philip Bernard couldn't have killed Marshall Lowe."

"Why not?"

"Because Bernard filled his pockets with debris from bomb sites and jumped off a bridge into the Thames early yesterday morning. Poor fool drowned before he was pulled out," Inspector Dawson told me. "Now please, move out of the way before I have to arrest you, too."

Then he was dead before I searched his room that morning. I felt guilty and I hoped the police didn't find out what I had done. Not that I had done any harm to their investigation, but I didn't think they'd see it that way.

A moment later, Si was on his feet with the two taller policemen on either side as they walked past me. I saw the handcuffs and cringed. "Call Sir Henry. He'll know what to do. And make sure the paper goes to press on time. I'm innocent," Si said in a pleading voice.

They marched him out, his bald head soaked with sweat.

I picked up the receiver and dialed Sir Henry's number.

Once we both got over the shock and Sir Henry was caught up on the broad outlines of what had happened, he said he'd send a reporter to Scotland Yard to find out the official version. "Perhaps it is time for me to call in a favor with Sir Malcolm," he added.

That was the last thing I wanted to hear. Sir Malcolm would probably send me to Canada or South Africa. "Oh, no. I have no intention of leaving London. And Marshall Lowe might have been loathsome, but he wasn't a Nazi spy."

"I simply plan to call in a favor. My goal is to have Sir Malcolm convince Scotland Yard that you should assist them in their investigation."

"Me?" My voice squeaked before I considered his plan and decided it might be interesting to see a police investigation from the inside for once.

"You. Si seems to trust you."

"If he trusted me, why was he going to the Regent Theatre behind my back? Was he following me to the other theaters?"

"That's something you'll be able to ask him if Sir Malcolm will talk Scotland Yard into having you on this investigation as his personal sleuth, reporting back to him. Or more accurately, me."

"What do you want me to do in the meantime?"

"Nothing." I could hear Sir Henry Benton's smile in his voice. "Let me work on Sir Malcolm first. Just carry on at *The Stage*."

That was easy to do. There was an incredible amount of work to be done to get that week's issue to the printer, and I was the only one available to do it.

* * *

It was that afternoon before I heard from Sir Henry at his desk on the top floor of the *Daily Premier*. "I've convinced Sir Malcolm, and he's convinced who knows whom at Scotland Yard. As soon as you can wrap up this day's work, get down there and ask to be directed to Inspector Dawson's office. And please, convince them to let you talk to Si on your own."

"Why is it so important to help Si?"

"I know he's innocent."

I growled through my teeth. "Try telling me something I might just believe. Such as the truth."

"We go back a long way. I know I can trust him. Otherwise, I'd never have sent you to him as his assistant."

I suspected there was more, but I knew I'd never get it today. "I'll go to Scotland Yard before I go home tonight. Can you send me someone down here who can handle the ads and the bookkeeping? Si handled all that on his own. I can take care of everything else."

"I'll have someone down there first thing in the

morning," Sir Henry promised.

I made speedy work of finishing up as much of the copy as I could and then hurried over to Scotland Yard. The inspector was in his office and I was led upstairs much the way I was when I visited Sir Malcolm, except the young man was in a police uniform instead of an army one.

"Mr. Chapell must have some powerful friends to have Sir Malcolm Freemantle insisting that you be seconded to my investigation," the inspector told me.

"It might be he has powerful enemies, or powerful secrets," I suggested.

Inspector Dawson studied me from where he sat behind his battered wooden desk as if he were judging my words. "Perhaps," he finally said. "Do not impede my investigation or you'll find yourself in a cell next to Mr. Chapell. Agreed?"

"Yes. What has Mr. Chapell told you?"

Dawson raised his eyebrows. "Only that he didn't kill Marshall Lowe, but that he deserved killing."

"May I speak with him? Alone?"

"No."

"May I speak with him?"

"I'll consider it."

"In the meantime, who else are you investigating?" I gave him as piercing a look as I could. I wanted into his investigation.

"No one."

"What? You can't have decided on Mr. Chapell and ruled everyone else out, because he didn't do it. You haven't even started to investigate this murder." I had raised my voice, but the inspector's raised eyebrows made me lower it again. Still, he couldn't be that foolish.

"Then who should I be looking at?" he asked in a challenging tone.

"So far, any relatives of Philip Bernard. But I intend to spend time at the Regent and see what I can learn. More than one person has said Marshall Lowe was a terrible person. And yes, I will let them know I am working with you."

"That won't make you popular."

"They may find it easier to talk to me than to you. I'm not frightening. You're—intimidating."

"Me? I'm mild-mannered." He gave me a ferocious grin.

"I don't think you rose to the rank of inspector by being mild-mannered."

"Think what you want. Simon Chapell killed Marshall Lowe and I will prove it, and you won't stand in my way."

"I will if you're wrong." I threw out the words as a challenge.

"What if I'm right?"

"Then it won't hurt you to let me speak to him."

"We'll speak to him together." There was his ferocious grin again. "In the meantime, we need to take your fingerprints."

"Why?"

"You told us you handled the director's tea mug. I wonder where else your fingerprints will show up." The inspector took me down the hall to record my digits.

He didn't seem too worried about it, for which I was grateful. But he didn't know I'd searched the playwright's room.

Chapter Twelve

Afterward, Inspector Dawson escorted me down corridors and stairs until we reached the holding cells in the cellar. It was cold, damp, and smelled vaguely of old cabbage. The windows were high up in the walls and barred, letting in a little light but no air.

When we were taken into an interview room, Si was waiting for us, looking shrunken within his clothes. Inspector Dawson gestured for me to sit across the table from Si before he sat next to me. The chair I chose rocked slightly, as if one leg was short.

I doubted any chair the inspector sat in would dare act that way.

Taking a deep breath, I tried to stare into Si's eyes, but he looked away. "How are you doing?" I asked him.

"This place is creepy. I hear moans and screams. The food is foul, the air is foul, the wardens are foul. For heaven's sake, Livvy, get me out of here."

"You've only been here a few hours," I reminded him.

"I look around," the inspector said, "and the only person I see with a motive is you."

"No. No. Other people wanted him dead."

"I'm waiting for names."

"Really. You want me to do your job for you?" Si looked disgusted. "I have my own job to do. Livvy, have you…"

Inspector Dawson interrupted. "I don't know the people at the Regent Theatre. You do. You've been spending enough time there."

"Unless you were there to keep an eye on me," I said to Si.

"No. I trust you, Livvy."

"Then tell me what you know about the people at the theater and why you were at the theater," I said. "It's likely someone there killed Lowe. Do you want to hang in their place?"

Si thought for about thirty seconds before he said, "Bud Cosby. He was all lined up to direct a comedy and play the lead when a rumor started that the accounts on his last musical didn't balance. Money was missing from the till. And guess who started the rumor as well as grabbed the director's job from him?"

"Marshall Lowe?" I asked.

"How can you be so sure that Lowe started the rumor?" the inspector asked.

"Cosby was sure it was Lowe. By the time the producer announced there was no money missing, Lowe was the new director and another actor, a friend of Lowe's, was starring in the show."

"How long ago was this?" I asked.

"Two years ago."

"Doesn't sound as if it is much of a motive to me," the inspector said.

"The play was that year's most highly anticipated. And Lowe also humiliated Marnie Keller."

"Marnie? She's a very nice woman. Why would he humiliate her?" I asked.

"Because he could." When I stared at him, he said, "You didn't hear this from me, but Lowe wanted to have an affair with Marnie. After she rebuffed him, he then rejected her publicly. Called her too old to play the lead in the next play he was putting on. Told her she should retire while she still had half her brain left and a tenth of her looks."

Good grief. What a horrid man. "Did he have lots of affairs with actresses?"

"Yes. All the time."

"Who was his current 'friend'?" I asked.

"Gloria Snelling. That just started. Before that, it was Jane Barber."

"Who plays the second daughter opposite Gloria, who plays the first daughter. And I suppose he dropped Jane just as publicly as Marnie."

"No, he didn't. Well, he didn't do it as an announcement to cast and crew this time. Just a heated argument in the dressing room, but everyone could hear them the whole way to the back of the balcony."

"And then there was Philip Bernard or any of his loved ones," I reminded him.

"Why do you mention him again?" Inspector Dawson

asked.

I reminded the inspector about the passage of the play from tragedy to comedy, ending with Bernard hanging around the Regent Theatre since Lowe's current play had returned to the West End, starting verbal and physical fights and finally being banned from the theater the day before Lowe was killed.

"Bernard has been a Londoner all his life. The murder, the trial, everything in his play took place in the East End. He wrote the play as an adult, perhaps to gain some perspective on his terrible childhood. Then he met Marshall Lowe and sold him the play. And I suspect he regretted it ever since," I finished.

"The play was changed and he didn't care for it? Hardly a reason to murder," the inspector said. "Especially for anyone else. Philip Bernard couldn't have done it."

Before he could say anything else, I replied, "This was the story of his childhood. How he was tortured and his mother was murdered and the wrong person hanged. To tamper with that so completely must have galled Bernard. Plus, I think there must have been insanity in the family."

"You still think that Philip Bernard was the killer?" the inspector asked, looking at me sideways.

"He had the strongest motive, plus he'd been most openly violent with Marshall Lowe. I would think he'd be your most promising suspect, if he were still alive."

"What if I were to remind you Bernard drowned in the Thames sometime the night before?" Inspector Dawson told us.

"Perhaps Bernard put the rat poison in the tea mug before he drowned and then Lowe didn't drink out of the mug until the next evening?" Si suggested.

"No. Lowe was seen to drink from his mug that morning when he first arrived at the theater. Cyanide is much too fast acting to have taken all day. Fifteen minutes is about all the time Lowe would have had." The inspector studied us carefully.

"Thank you, Inspector. That's certainly clear," I told him, feeling slightly ill at the thought. "Lowe paid Bernard for the play, is that correct?" I asked Si.

"And paid handsomely, according to rumor, once Bernard finished the asked-for rewrites and Lowe and the company returned from this tour. Who inherits, Inspector?"

"I have no idea. If he had any money left."

"He hadn't spent it. He was ill-dressed, ill-fed, and ill-housed from the looks of him. I would suggest checking the banks to see where he deposited the money," I said.

"East Enders tend not to trust banks," Si said. "You think he could have hidden it?"

"Yes." I couldn't think of any other logical answer. "He went out to kill himself. He'd have wanted the money safe for whoever he wanted to give it to."

"It wasn't found on his body," Inspector Dawson said. "Or near it. We checked. And we've been through his room in his rooming house."

After a moment while I wondered when they'd been

through his room and if they had learned that I had, I asked, "Any other possibilities for our killer at the Regent, Si?"

"Just petty rivalries. Lowe insulted the craftsmen by not letting them use the electric kettle that he said was for the actors' use only. He was rude to everyone. Ian Nelson is the producer, but Lowe treated his rules as suggestions and made a hash of his budgets."

"Nelson handles the purse strings?" I asked.

"Yes, and Lowe overspent and then handed him the bills to be paid as if the producer was a bottomless pit of funds."

"Did he treat all his producers that way, or was it only Nelson?"

"All of them. The same way all ingenue actresses were fair game for his pursuit. All writers would have their plays revised beyond recognition. And every year, he'd get more brazen. He believed his own publicity." Si rested his chin on his hands with his elbows propped on the table.

"Then why didn't the play run into nasty attacks when it played at other theaters in other towns?" There had to be a reason this all started on the play's return to London.

"I don't know," Si told me. "There wasn't any trouble anywhere on the tour."

"And you were in London the whole time?" Inspector Dawson asked.

"Yes. I have a paper to put out every week almost singlehandedly."

"So, you didn't have access to Lowe or the play until it came to London." He stared at Si.

"Well, no." Si looked uncomfortable and started to sweat again.

"Philip Bernard was from London and was around the theater once rehearsals started here," I said.

"And you think the person who pulled the nasty tricks wasn't the person who killed Lowe?" Inspector Dawson said.

"I think a close relative could be involved," I replied. "Who inherits?"

"No idea. Good grief," the inspector said, turning to Si. "Why don't you tell us how this feud between you and Marshall Lowe began."

Si shook his head and pursed his lips together.

"If I can get rid of the inspector, would you tell me?" I asked.

The look the inspector gave me was chilling.

"You'd just tell him. He'd make you, and you'd have to tell him. And I don't want anyone to know." Si glared at me as if this was somehow my fault.

"We'll find out sooner or later. It would go better for you if you just told us," the inspector said.

"There's no way you're going to find out." Si crossed his arms and stared back at the policeman.

"Why were you hanging around the Regent Theatre? Didn't you trust my reporting?" I asked.

"Of course, I trusted you. Sir Henry sent you over, didn't he?" He uncrossed his arms as he focused on me.

"Yes."

"That's good enough recommendation for me. I trust Sir

Henry, and I trust you."

"Then why were you over there? I was covering the theaters currently hosting plays."

"Never you mind, Livvy. It had nothing to do with you or the job you were doing." Once again, he crossed his arms and shut his mouth.

We tried a little longer but got nowhere. As we rose to leave, Si said, "How did Bernard drown? The official report?"

"He filled his pockets with rocks and building debris weighing over ten pounds and then went to the middle of Waterloo Bridge and went over the railing. He was spotted, but by the time they fished him out, he was dead," the inspector said.

I shook my head in horror at the image. "And I suppose his ghost couldn't have killed Lowe."

"No, we are not going to consider murder by ghost. One more stupid suggestion similar to that and I am throwing you off this case, Sir Malcolm or no Sir Malcolm. Now, go," the inspector ordered.

Si winced. "And he didn't have any money worries. Something else was preying on his mind. If he was even sane."

As I turned to leave, Si told me, "Be sure to get the paper to the printer either tonight or tomorrow morning."

The inspector had me leave the interview room first, no doubt afraid I'd start talking about *The Stage* or pass a message.

When we returned to the inspector's office, he asked

me, "How did you manage not to see him at the Regent?"

"Are you certain he was often there? I was frequently in the wings where I could see the front of the house and the hallway to the dressing rooms and the stage door. I never saw him."

"That's what I've been told."

"Who told you that?"

"Old Nick."

"That makes no sense." I ran through my memories of the Regent. "Old Nick wasn't at his post half the time when I went in or out."

"He claims he has little hidey-holes around the theater where he watches the comings and goings of people. He saw Mr. Chapell almost daily. And Chapell and Lowe nearly came to blows once."

"All while I wasn't there?" I asked.

"Apparently."

"Who was he going to visit at the theater?"

"Various people."

"No, Inspector Dawson, that theory doesn't hold up. Since he wasn't covering anything there for the newspaper, he must have had a very specific person or reason for going there, especially almost daily."

"Maybe he told you a fib and he really was going there to check up on your work."

"Then he would have been there to listen to my interviews and I would have seen him. No, there's more to Si being there than you've found out so far."

"That's possible. I'm going back to the theater tomorrow morning. Meet me there at ten and we'll find out." When I didn't move, he added, "Good night, Mrs. Redmond."

"Are you going to check Marshall Lowe's bank records and find out when he paid Philip Bernard for the play and how much?"

He gave me that ferocious smile of his. "It'll be done before I see you at the theater."

"Good night, Inspector Dawson."

* * *

My father was already sitting at the dinner table when I arrived at his house after a scorching hot, jolting ride on the Underground. "Go upstairs and clean up," he greeted me. "We can reheat your dinner afterward."

"Good evening, Father." I trudged up the stairs and poured myself a bath. I have to admit it felt good after all I'd been through that day.

I went back downstairs to find my father had just finished reheating soup. It didn't taste very good, but it filled me up. "That's all I want. Thank you."

"What about your dinner?"

"I'm hot. I'm tired. My new boss has just been arrested for murder. I have no appetite. Do with it what you want."

"Well, I won't let it go to waste." The portion was small enough that he finished it off within minutes while I went into the kitchen and did the dishes.

When he finished, my father brought out his plates for me to wash and said, "There's a letter from Adam on the drawing room mantel for you."

That was my father's preferred place for Mrs. Johnson to leave letters when she brought in the mail. I raced through the dishes and then quickly dried my hands on a dishtowel before rushing into the drawing room.

I immediately sat down and read his letter twice. All was well. He missed me. He hoped my new newspaper position was working out all right. After the war, he wanted to show me the place he currently was stationed for its scenic beauty.

Folding the letter, I put it in my pocket. Then I went back to the kitchen to dry the dishes and put them away.

"Adam have anything to say for himself?" my father asked.

"That he's well and he misses me. Apparently, right now he's in a beautiful spot that he wants to show me after the war."

"When you write him back, give him my regards." He left the kitchen to go into his study.

When I finished, I went upstairs to my room—well, our room now that I shared it with Adam—and wrote him. All was well, I missed him, and we had a murder at one of the theaters I was covering. My new boss was suspected of the killing, but I didn't think so. My true boss, Sir Henry, had me helping find the real killer.

I hoped all that got through the censors.

Before I sealed up the letter, I wrote that my father wished Adam well. As long as I was going to filch a stamp off my father, I should at least do as he asked and mention that he sent Adam his regards.

Then I went back downstairs and into my father's study. It was only a moment before I had a stamp on my letter and it was ready to be posted.

"I suppose I'll have to buy more stamps," my father said, looking up from the newspaper he was reading in his well-cushioned chair.

"If you would, that would be helpful," I told him.

"How long will you be living here?" he asked, eyebrows raised.

Here it was. I tried to act as if it didn't hurt. "I don't know. It depends on the war, Adam's assignments, my assignments. And how long until new housing can be built." I gestured with my palms held out facing him.

"I'm praying for a short war. Maybe now that the Germans have invaded Russia, it will be a very short war. One Russian winter and Hitler should be finished." With a self-satisfied sigh, my father returned to his newspaper.

Chapter Thirteen

After a night spent tossing and turning, trying to think of a witty response that would put my father in his place, I rose with the realization that no matter what I said, my father didn't want me around. And that hurt.

Breakfast was a silent affair as usual. When I asked my father if there was anything interesting in the newspaper, he didn't bother answering. I thanked Mrs. Johnson for breakfast and walked to the Underground station, leaving my father in peace.

I had agreed to meet the inspector at the Regent Theatre that morning, but even after I stopped at *The Stage* office and went to the printer's shop with this week's copy, I arrived first. Deciding not to waste time, I went in search of anyone who might be there that early.

The young woman costumer sat on the old sofa backstage with a stack of clothing next to her and a shirt and needle and thread in her lap.

I walked over and introduced myself. "I'm Livvy Redmond from *The Stage*. I've seen you sitting here working a couple of times. Including the first act of opening night."

"I'm Millie. I'm a costumer. And this spot has the best lighting in the entire theater. You've heard about the slashed costumes?" She was in her early twenties, with dark hair and eyes, and pretty enough to be an actress.

"Yes. That's left you with a lot of work." I pointed to the clothes next to her.

"And this is only part of the damage."

"Good luck getting all that done," I said. "Now, the first act Tuesday night. Did you see anyone around Lowe's tea mug?"

"No."

"No? You were sitting right there with a clear view of the tea mugs."

"I was doing emergency repairs on a costume in the women's dressing room for most of the first act. There was over half an hour when I wasn't anywhere near the teapot."

"Did you see anyone while you were sitting out here?"

"Just Lowe."

"All right. Thanks."

The electricians were up in the scaffolding working on the lights. "Hello," I called from the stage. "You're here early."

"Cosby doesn't care for the lighting the way Lowe wanted it, so we have to set up everything differently," the younger man called down.

"Is he changing anything else, or is it all falling on you?"

"The stagehands will be here soon to change some of the staging. The actors will be learning some new lines before lunch time, and the costumers and the props man have some minor changes to work into the play," the younger one said.

"So, we're not the only ones affected by Lowe's death," the older man called down.

"But who wanted him dead?" I asked.

"Who knows?" the older man said.

"My money's on the actors," the younger man said.

"Which one?"

"Doesn't matter," he replied.

"Why?"

"They were the ones who had to deal with him, day in and day out. We just had to repair things once in a while."

I thanked them and went back to the dressing rooms to see if anyone had come in early. I found a woman sewing in Marnie Keller's dressing room.

"Hi, I'm Livvy Redmond. And you are?"

"Too busy to talk to you," the woman grumbled. She was perhaps in her fifties, the same as Marnie, but very plain in her dress and she didn't wear any makeup.

I decided to take a shot in the dark. "Do you know Si Chapell?"

"Yeah. What of it?"

"He's been arrested for the murder of Marshall Lowe. Any idea why?"

"Arrested?" She stopped sewing. "Why?"

"That's what I'm trying to find out."

"Well, you won't find out in here."

"I won't find out if people don't start telling me what

they know." Frustrated, I began to pace the dressing room. When I glimpsed a display of flowers with the telegrams, I slipped out the card. The large display of roses was sent with the words "All my love, S.C."

"So, Si has feelings for Marnie," I said.

The woman snatched the card out of my hand. "That's private."

"Nothing's private in a murder investigation," came from the doorway. I turned to see the inspector staring at the woman, his sergeant behind him. "I'm Inspector Dawson and this is Sergeant Mullins from Scotland Yard. What's your name and role in this theater?"

"I'm Nora Brent, and I'm Miss Keller's dresser."

"Dresser?" the inspector asked.

"The aristocracy has lady's maids, actresses have dressers. At least the aristocracy of actresses." She picked up her sewing and put in a few more stitches to finish the hem in a dress and set it aside. "Now, what do you want to know? I have plenty to keep me busy. And you should too."

"Continue on while we talk," Inspector Dawson said. "Did you see much of Marshall Lowe?"

Nora rose and hung up the dress she'd been repairing on the rack before picking up another and sitting back down. Only then did she say, "I saw very little of him, which suited me just fine."

"Why was that?"

"Because I'm a dresser, not an actor." She started picking out stitches in the bodice of another dress.

"No, why did that suit you?"

"He wasn't a nice man."

"How do you know he wasn't a nice man if you saw very little of him?" I asked.

"He was rude to everyone. He was rude to Marnie, and she was unfailingly polite to him. She's a star, and he was nothing more than a second-rate director."

"He was also the author of the play they are putting on here."

"Which he stole." She stopped then. "That's not quite right. He bought it for a good sum, rewrote it as a comedy, and didn't give the original writer any credit. Typical of him, not to give anyone else any credit."

"Had Marnie worked in a play with Marshall Lowe before this one?"

"Yes. *Bells and Whistles.* Her big success three years ago. He was so awful she swore she'd never work with the swine again. Always on her about her age, her weight, her singing."

"I didn't know Marnie was a singer," I told her, surprised at all I was learning.

"She is, but when it came to this play with Marshall Lowe, she refused to sing. She's got a beautiful voice. But the only way Ian—Ian Nelson, the producer—could sign her was to put in the contract, no singing. That and pay her extra to put up with the swine."

"Did she have any reason to want the extra money, even if it meant putting up with the swine?" I asked.

"She has a cottage in the Cotswolds. Wants to fix it up,

but everything costs so dear with the war on. The money for this show will go a long way to paying for modernizing it."

That at least rang true. "And after this play? What does she have lined up next?"

"That depends on how long this goes on."

"You've been around a lot of plays and a lot of theaters, I imagine." I wanted to get her talking.

"All your life." She dismissed me with three words.

I was going to keep trying. "How much longer do you think this play will run?"

"With Bud Cosby directing and starring and Marnie starring? Might run until the end of the year, if the bombing doesn't return. Pass me that basket behind you."

I did and saw more colors of thread when she opened it.

"When is Miss Keller coming into the theater today?" the inspector asked.

"Noon. She and Cosby will be working on a few tweaks for the show, now that Lowe is out of the way."

"What do you mean, 'out of the way'?" the inspector asked, straightening from where he lounged against the wall.

"He's dead, isn't he?"

"How convenient." His tone dripped sarcasm.

"Yes, and that's all there is to it." She lowered the sewing to her lap. "Neither Miss Keller nor Mr. Cosby would kill anyone, especially a second-rate talent such as Marshall Lowe."

"But they have the best motives," I said.

"Look at the women in this play. Not Miss Keller, but the

others. What do they all have in common? Start by looking there." She went back to her sewing. "Now leave me in peace."

The inspector and the sergeant left and I followed. I heard voices down the hallway that the policemen were striding toward. When I arrived, I found them talking to a young man and woman I'd seen around the theater before.

"Who are you?" the inspector was asking them.

"Diana Carroll, third daughter," the young woman said. Up close, she was older than I realized, perhaps in her mid-twenties, the same as Jane Barber and Gloria Snelling. With her blonde hair in braids, she appeared younger than her two "sisters" in the play.

"Michael Harris, love interest to third daughter and all-around leading man in a few years." He was perhaps in his early twenties, and I would have asked why he hadn't been called up for service yet except the sergeant beat me to it.

"A dodgy ticker," the young man answered. "They decided I'd be of more use to the national interest by entertaining people than defending them."

"Born with it, were you?" Sergeant Mullins continued, sounding skeptical.

"Yes." Michael gave him a wide-toothed smile.

"Had Marshall Lowe been making advances to you?" the inspector asked Diana.

"I only joined recently when the other actress broke her leg in the dance scene. He started in on me almost immediately. Before that he was having an affair with Jane

Barber. When she heard him trying it on with me, she dumped him loud enough for all of us to hear." It was her turn to give Inspector Dawson a bright smile.

"We've heard he had an affair with her," I said.

"Yes, and good luck to her. He was a tightwad."

"Such as?"

"Offering an extra shilling a week for my role in the play to sleep with him. And it wouldn't even be his money. It would be the play's money. The producer pays our salaries."

Her statement was so shocking that the policemen had no idea how to respond. I blurted out, "I wonder why he wasn't murdered before now."

Diana laughed. "There are a lot the same as him in the theater. Just usually, they aren't so cheap or so blatant. Nobody would have killed him over an offer such as that."

"What did he do when you turned him down?"

"Nothing. Said it was my loss and he wouldn't hire me again. I reminded him he hadn't hired me this time."

"Who had?" I asked.

"The producer, Ian Nelson. He put together a deal for a touring production to play so many towns and so many military facilities with the government before coming to London. He found the director and through him the play, the actors, and was given a budget. The MOD found the theaters in every town, including the Regent." Michael Harris spoke as if this was common knowledge.

"Did the MOD specify a comedy?"

"Yes, they almost always do. And then Lowe went to

Nelson with his play. No one knew then that he had bought it from Bernard and rewritten it," Harris answered.

"When did you learn Lowe had rewritten the play? Or bought it off someone else?" I asked.

Harris smiled and said, "We were in the first or second day of rehearsals after we returned to London when a thin young man who needed a haircut and a shave came in and started yelling at Marshall. Marshall yelled back and convinced the stagehands to escort him out of the theater so we could continue.

"We were rehearsing here, in the Regent," Harris continued. "The head stagehand, Gil Baker, listened to more of his story than most of us and when I asked Baker, he said the man's name was Philip Bernard, that he'd written the original play, and it was a tragedy. The story of his childhood."

Diana continued the tale. "We asked Marshall about it, and he said not to worry about it, the play was his, and we had all we could handle learning our lines."

"Never very flattering," I said. "Did you see Bernard again?"

"Yes," Michael said.

"Daily," Diana said.

"But I haven't seen him since Lowe died. He must know," Harris said.

"Perhaps he killed him," Diana added.

"He did pull a kitchen knife on him less than a week ago," Harris said.

"Good heavens," I gasped.

"Where is the knife now?" the inspector asked.

"I have no idea. It was Old Nick who convinced him to hand over the knife. We were all running away and hiding," Michael said. "Including Lowe."

"Are you certain? You said you ran and hid," the sergeant said. Mullins didn't sound impressed with any of the actors or their bravery.

"Lowe hid behind the scenery with me," Michael said. "If Bernard had come back there to find us, I would have put Lowe in front of me as a shield."

"Not advisable, sir," the inspector said. "It seldom works as it's shown in the moving pictures."

"Was Si Chapell around here at that time? The editor of *The Stage?*" I asked.

"Oh, we know who he is. Marnie's boyfriend," Michael said.

"At least he fancies himself as her beau," Diana said.

Was that what he'd been hiding? It seemed as if it was such a silly secret to try to hide from the police. It sounded as if the entire cast of the play knew, and even if he was embarrassed by his infatuation with Marnie, it was no reason to keep quiet and languish in a jail cell.

I looked at the inspector and said, "I wonder if that is what Si is keeping to himself. It would hardly be a reason to kill Marshall Lowe."

"I doubt that's his big secret." The inspector smirked.

"Then what is it?" I was certain Si was innocent of

murder, but what was he trying to keep quiet? Being in love with Marnie Keller was hardly a reason to stay locked up in a prison.

"I think you'll find he's hiding the fact he put the rat poison in Marshall Lowe's tea. A secret he'll hang for."

"Would someone who pulled a knife on a man then later come back and kill him with rat poison?" Harris asked.

"Of course not. Bernard couldn't have killed him that way," Inspector Dawson said.

"Why not?" Harris asked. "He certainly seemed ready to kill Lowe."

"Because Bernard drowned himself in the Thames before the time it was possible the rat poison was added to Lowe's teacup," the inspector said.

"Blimey," Harris said.

"If Bernard didn't do it," Diana asked, "who did? And who gets all that money Bernard received for the play now that he's gone?"

"Yeah," Harris said. "Didn't all of his family die thanks to his grandmother?"

"How much did Lowe pay him for the play?" I asked.

Both Diana and Michael shrugged with moves that could be seen in the balcony.

"Everyone in the cast would love to get their hands on that money," Diana said. "Inspector, have your men found it?"

"Not yet," the inspector said, sounding embarrassed at their failure.

Diana and Michael looked at each other and said in unison, "Treasure hunt."

"No," Inspector Dawson said. "That money belongs to the estate of Philip Bernard and must be turned into Scotland Yard if found. Anyone who takes it and tries to spend it will be charged with theft and go to prison for years."

"Oh, inspector, you're such a party pooper," Diana said. She walked off giggling, arm in arm with Michael.

"I don't think you got through to them," I told the policeman.

"If they start spending money beyond their salaries, we'll have them," the sergeant muttered.

"How much did Lowe pay Bernard for the play?"

The inspector told me, and I nearly choked.

"You found the contract?"

"The contract, the bank details, everything. And Bernard insisted on being paid in cash just four days before his death."

"Wait a minute. That makes no sense," I told him. "They've been putting on *Have You Seen My Mother-in-Law?* for nearly a year."

"What we've been told is the truth. Lowe wrote the comedy and put it on while negotiating with Bernard for a play to put on after the war when tragedies would be in fashion again."

"Perhaps Lowe read Bernard's play last year, rewrote it into a comedy, and then a year later bought Bernard's play to put away for after the war. It still doesn't explain why both men were killed." We were missing something.

"Bernard killed himself. He was seen jumping off the bridge, and there was no one around him. Lowe was the only one murdered. Still, it doesn't explain either death."

"Why kill yourself after getting a fortune? Bernard was crazy," the sergeant said.

"Perhaps someone he knew stole it from him before his death. His fortune gone, he killed himself since he didn't see any other way out," I suggested.

"Anyone spending money they shouldn't have?" the inspector asked.

I shook my head. "Or maybe he's just hidden it really, really well."

Chapter Fourteen

Voices were heard at the stage door, and then Bud Cosby came in saying, "Don't tell me. Old Nick has disappeared again. I need to speak to the owners of the theater about a replacement."

"Oh, you can't. Old Nick has been a fixture here for years." I recognized the modulated tones of a stage-trained voice. Marnie Keller.

I was beginning to notice that all of the actors in this play, including the youngsters in Diana and Harris, said everything so it could be heard in the back of the balcony.

The inspector walked over and said something quietly to Cosby. I could hear Cosby's reply clearly. "We need to have a rehearsal to iron out the wrinkles in this play. Very well, just make it quick."

It was Sergeant Mullins who barked out, "Everybody, actors, backstage workers, come out here for the inspector. Now, please. Everybody to the front of the stage." You could hear him in the balcony, too.

I stood to one side and watched Nora Brent come out with Marnie Keller. The actors grouped themselves around Bud Cosby. The electricians and stagehands stood off to the sides as if distancing themselves from the actors. The dressers stood behind the actors they worked for, more than one with sewing in their hands. Ian Nelson came down to the front of the house. Old Nick stood in the shadows by the backstage door. The actor I knew as Vic Graybell, with his shaky hands, stood in the shadows of the backstage curtain.

"You are all aware by now that your director died by poisoning. While we have someone locked up on suspicion, we are not convinced the danger is past. Therefore, we're going to have a police presence backstage for every rehearsal and performance and we'll post a guard at the stage door."

Inspector Dawson gazed around him and then added, "If anyone sees or has seen anything odd, please bring it to the attention of any police officer. In the meantime, we'll be stopping and questioning members of the cast and the stagehands if we have any follow-up questions. Thank you."

"Thank you, Inspector," Cosby said, as the spokesman for the actors.

The electricians and stagehands as well as the props and sound men walked away, presumably back to their tasks. The producer came up onto the stage and spoke in low tones to the inspector.

I walked over to the actor, Vic, who was trying to disappear into the curtains. "I'm sorry. I'm not sure of your name. Is it Vic? Vic Graybell?"

"Yes. Victor Graybell. I play the second son-in-law."

"You seem awfully shy for an actor."

"I was sent to France with the army as a translator.

Then— things—fell apart."

"I know. My husband was over there." And still walked with crutches because of the fighting in France.

"He made it back?"

"Wounded, but he returned from Cherbourg."

"He was lucky. I saw more death than I was prepared for in three or four lifetimes." He slowly shook his head.

"You must have returned and gone right into this play."

"Yes. When they saw how much I shake, they decided I could go back on the stage. I'm no good for the army. Or anything else."

"And now your director is murdered," I reminded him.

"My shaking's become worse again. I thought I was recovered, at least to get on and off the stage, but now…" He pulled his hands out from behind the curtains so I could now see how badly he trembled.

"Did anything help you before?" I asked.

"Only time." He took a deep breath.

"You have all the time you need here. Try to get plenty of rest between performances. I'm sure it will help you again," I told him and turned away to meet the props man.

I found him in the props storeroom, an enclosed cupboard near the far side of the stage. The man working in there was well past conscription age, chunky, with thinning hair and pale blue eyes. His clothes were not only cleaned, but pressed. "Excuse me, Mr.-?" I asked.

"Bert Lanshire. How can I help you?"

"I'm Livvy Redmond from *The*—"

"I know where you're from. We all do. What we don't know is how you got mixed up with the police."

"They arrested my boss, Si Chapell, for the murder. I've latched myself onto the police to prove he didn't do it."

"I can see why you'd want to do that. Si is a nice person." He studied me for a long moment, as if he couldn't decide if I were trustworthy or not. "I can't see why the police would be willing to have you tag along."

"The same people who assigned me to work on *The Stage* have some sway with Scotland Yard. Now, how long have you been working with this group?"

"Since casting calls went out for the tour. I've worked with Nelson a few times, Marnie a few times, Cosby a few times. The theater is a small community in this country. We've all met each other here and there."

"You went on tour with them?"

"Of course. Left my wife seeing after our pub while I was gone. Went traveling with my second wife," he said and patted a large steamer trunk. "All the props travel in Bessie here."

He named the props trunk "Bessie"? Mr. Lanshire was a lighthearted man. "I thought you must be married," I told him.

"Why? Is it my hangdog expression?"

I laughed as he meant for me to. "You're the only one here with brushed and pressed clothing."

He chuckled and patted his stomach. "She does look after me well."

"How long have you known Marnie?"

"Since she was a lass. Pretty thing, too. A few years before the Great War."

I did the math quickly. "She must have been very young then."

"About the same age as me. Or your parents. We were all young then. And then the war took it away."

"It?"

"Our youth. Don't let this war take your youth away from you." He shook his head. "Anything else you want to know?"

"Who killed Marshall Lowe?"

"Could have been anyone. No one liked him, but I didn't think anyone disliked him enough to murder."

"Someone did. Has anyone done anything suspicious?"

"No. I don't think so." Lanshire shook his head again. "Mind you, that Bernard chap could have killed him when he saw what Lowe had done to his play. And he kept on and on, working himself up. He could have done it, except he topped himself."

A vague idea came to me. "Had Bernard written anything for the theater before?"

"No. Nothing that's been staged."

There went that idea. I thought perhaps Bernard had written something for Lowe prior to this play.

"He was a small-part actor for a couple of years before the war," the props man told me.

"Bernard was?"

"Yes." Lanshire gestured me to take a chair while he sat

on a large wooden crate.

"Why hadn't anyone mentioned this to me before?"

"I don't know. It wasn't any secret. But he wasn't well known. Just bit parts here and there. I happen to remember him from a play I was props man on because of something that happened, not because of Bernard's acting ability."

"What happened to make him memorable?"

"We were using an antique letter opener that belonged to the great-grandfather of the director. The letter opener was highly ornate, very beautiful. It went missing one day shortly after Bernard was seen standing by the table, and he was accused of taking it. He denied it and challenged the director to call the police. He also attacked the fellow actor who said he was seen by the props table."

"Had he taken it?" I couldn't wait to hear the rest of the story.

"No. The opener had apparently been stolen and pawned. The police found it and arrested a stagehand with a criminal record along with an employee of the pawn shop. It turned out they had worked together to steal it for money, each blaming the other."

"And that's why you remembered Bernard had been an actor."

"Yes, and I'm sure Lowe remembered him, too. Lowe was the director on that play. It was his letter opener."

"Who else working on this play was in that one as well?"

He shrugged. "I don't recall. It was three or four years ago."

"Be sure to tell that story to the inspector. He needs to hear it."

"Why?" It was Lanshire's turn to question me.

"Because it shows another motive. Another side to Lowe's character as a collector of beautiful things."

"Beautiful things. Beautiful people," Lanshire murmured.

"Did you say something?" I asked. I wasn't sure I'd heard correctly.

"Me? Not a word."

"Bert? You got any cable in there? I need to fix one of the speakers." The man who squeezed into the cupboard with us was in worn trousers, a collarless shirt, and braces.

"This is Mac. Our soundman. The guardian of our record," Bert said.

"Had to replace it out of me own money. Daft saboteur, or ghost. When I catch up with them…" Mac walked over and picked up a spool of wire.

"Our dance music from act one disappeared one day, a few days before Wanda broke her leg. Mac was not best pleased," Bert said.

"I'll bring this back," Mac said, walking away.

"I do have to get back to work." Bert turned his back on me and began fiddling with some crockery used in the first act.

I left his crowded space and went to see how things were going on stage. Marnie was going through her lines, setting up her plan as the matriarch of the family to see if they had really inherited a castle and to test her three daughters to see if they loved her. Unlike *King Lear*, this was a rollicking comedy, and confusion, jokes, and loud, good-natured fun would be the result in this play.

Bud Cosby, in his new role as actor/director, was trying out some changes to the lines and moving Marnie and Vic Graybell, who was playing the second son-in-law, around the stage. I could see at once why. Before, they'd just stood there talking. Now there was some movement as well as a little more humor. Cosby was improving what was already a good play.

"Vic, I want you to show the audience some warmth," Bud said.

"Warmth?" Vic asked. I could see his hand was shaking.

"You've got a beautiful wife, a mother-in-law who wants to hug the stuffing out of you, and we all want to laugh together."

"Laugh?" Vic shook his head. "Laugh?" He sounded slightly hysterical.

"Sure, you know how badly everyone needs to laugh. Let's give our audience what they need. I know you can do it."

"But Lowe…"

"Lowe's not here. I am. And I know you can do it. You have a talent for making us believe the words you are saying. How much you trust Marnie. I have faith you can carry this off. Now let's do it." Bud slapped Vic on the back and prompted them into the rest of the scene.

The rest of the cast was sitting in the front of the house watching the scene or reading their newly changed scripts. The electricians came over to stand by me in the wings.

"Now I see why he wants the lighting change," the younger electrician whispered to the other. Then he turned to me. "Have you finished with the police yet?"

"I doubt it," I said, thinking of how long I'd have to work with them to find the solution to who had finally had enough of Marshall Lowe. "What were they asking you?"

"What we saw when Lowe was around. Did he owe us money? Threaten us or our families. All stuff that will get them nowhere."

"Why was he killed? Do you know?"

"It's got to have something to do with the producer. Those two couldn't be in the same room without Lowe ordering Nelson around. It's supposed to be the other way," the younger electrician said.

"Why was Nelson letting Lowe order him around?" I asked.

"Blackmail." He nodded emphatically. "Blackmail."

"What about?"

"Some show they both worked on just before the war. The war started and all the theaters closed immediately. Then within weeks they sent plays out into the rest of the country. Men were drafted in greater numbers. Everything was chaos. It took time to find out that money from the production they had been working on before the start of the war was missing. At least, they thought so. The books didn't balance. Somebody didn't get paid. Or something."

"I take it you don't know the details," I said, staring at him.

"Well, no. But my mate who was a stagehand at the Green Park Theatre at the start of the war knows about it."

"Where is he now?"

He shrugged. "Somewhere in the army."

"In other words, it's all rumor," the older electrician said.

"The bookkeeper for the Green Park Theatre should be able to straighten out truth from fiction," I said.

At that moment, we saw the inspector follow the sergeant around the side of the front of the house and into the wings. "Time for a break," the older electrician said and headed for the stage door.

"Where's...?" I started to ask where Old Nick was, but the electricians moved rapidly away from me and down the hall to the stage door, leaving me to face the policemen alone. "Have you seen Old Nick?"

"No. We've been looking for him without any luck," Inspector Dawson said. "Who have you been talking to?"

"An actor, the props and sound men, and then the electricians."

"Learn anything?"

"Bernard, the author of the original play, and Lowe had a history going back a few years when Bernard was an actor in a play Lowe directed. An antique letter opener belonging to Lowe was stolen and Bernard was accused. The police were called and found where it had been pawned and jailed the thieves. Not Bernard."

Sergeant Mullins was scribbling furiously. Dawson said, "Anything else?"

"There's a rumor that a play both Nelson and Lowe worked on when the war started was missing money. The shortage didn't turn up for a while since things were chaotic. This happened at the Green Park Theatre. The rumor is Nelson was being blackmailed by Marshall Lowe because of the embezzlement." I studied the inspector for a moment. "Anything you'd care to share?"

"No."

I decided to try it a different way. "What have you learned that you don't want to share?"

Inspector Dawson cracked a smile. "That's police business."

"The same way it is police business to lock up the wrong man." I shared with them and they were hiding something that could be important in exonerating Si. I was annoyed with them and I showed it, which I shouldn't have.

"Maybe if your editor would tell us what he was doing here if it wasn't playing pranks and killing Lowe, we could make a start at finding another suspect."

"If you'd let me speak with him without the watchful eyes and ears of Scotland Yard, I might be persuaded to get him to talk." I wasn't certain by any means that it would work, but I still might accomplish more than the police had so far.

"No. I'm not going to let you carry out your own investigation under our noses."

"You'd rather risk hanging an innocent man than accept my help and the help of Sir Malcolm." I was glaring at the inspector.

"If it is help, which I doubt," Inspector Dawson responded.

"Has Si told you anything so far?"

"No."

"Then anything I can convince him to tell me, to tell you, is bound to be a help."

"It's bound to be half-truths, or lies. Nothing that would be a help." Inspector Dawson began to walk away from me. "I'm going to interview Marnie Keller. Would you care to come along?"

"Yes." I set off to follow Dawson and Mullins, only to find them stopped at her dressing room door by her dresser, Nora.

"You're not to enter here," she told them, her arms crossed.

"Stand aside," Dawson said, and Mullins carefully nudged Nora to the side.

The policemen opened the door to be greeted by a shriek that could have been heard in Westminster.

Chapter Fifteen

I squeezed around the inspector and into Marnie's private dressing room. She was in her corset and little else. I swung around and slammed the door in the policemen's faces, at which point the mezzo-soprano screams died down.

"Can I help?"

"Get Nora. Get my dresser. And keep those peeping toms away."

I nodded and opened the door enough to slip out. "Nora. You're wanted," I said and stood in front of the door until Nora was inside and the door was closed again.

"I don't think you're going to be very popular with Marnie Keller for quite a while," I told the policemen. "She's practically an institution, and you've insulted her badly. If the rest of the actors take her side, you won't get another word out of any of them."

"We are investigating a murder. I need to apologize to Miss Keller for walking in on her, but we need to speak," Inspector Dawson said.

"Why don't we interview someone else who is dressed and then come back?" I suggested.

The policemen walked away and I followed them. The

first person they came to was Robbie Day, sitting on a chair onstage memorizing his new lines. He looked up as we walked toward him and smiled. "You really upset Marnie, didn't you?"

"An unfortunate mistake," the inspector said, looking sheepish. "What can you tell me about Marshall Lowe's murder?"

"Nothing."

"Have you noticed anyone coming in or out of the storeroom in the corner beyond the stage door?" I asked him.

"Is that where the murder weapon was found?" Robbie asked me.

"There's plenty in there besides a weapon," I told him. "Who have you seen going in there?"

"Old Nick, of course. Also Michael Harris and Diana Carroll. And Art Jackson, of course."

"Why of course?" the sergeant asked.

"He's the building manager. This really is his building."

"Why were Michael Harris and Diana Carroll in there?" the sergeant continued.

"Looking for a little privacy?" I suggested. They were both young and might fancy each other almost as much as they fancied themselves.

"They were never in there at the same time." Robbie gave me a wide-eyed look.

"What are they up to?" the inspector asked. The sergeant was busily adding to his notes.

"I don't know," the actor replied with a headshake. "It

began since we came back to London. Shortly after Diana joined our troop."

"She hasn't been with you long," Sergeant Mullins offered in response.

"No. About a week."

"How did she join your play? It had been running for nearly a year at that point, hadn't it?" I prompted. I knew all that, but doubted the police did.

"You were here that day. Wanda Thomas broke her leg rehearsing the dance scene. Diana was the first one to show up here the very next day. But she's not the only one to join us recently."

"Really? Who?"

"Jane Barber.

"I thought she'd been here all along," I said.

"Not at all. The actress who had the second daughter role before was called up to take a job where she will use her language skills. Michael Harris said he knew someone perfect for the role who was available and he'd give her a whistle. Nelson met her, agreed, and she went on three days later."

"Did she know anyone in the cast beside Harris?" the inspector asked.

"I don't think so." Robbie shook his head. "No, I'm sure she didn't."

"How did she get along with Lowe?" I asked.

"A little harmless flirting. She did that with everyone, from our producer to the youngest stagehand."

"Inspector." A woman's voice called from behind where

I stood. We all turned to see Nora standing at the edge of the stage. "Miss Keller will see you now."

"Thank you," the inspector said with a slight bow and then followed her after thanking Robbie Day. Mullins went next and I brought up the rear.

The first few minutes in Marnie's dressing room were spent with the inspector groveling. I admired Marnie's forcing it upon him without seeming to. She was a theater veteran and I imagine this was part of her weaponry, honed over decades of combat.

The inspector kept the questioning light and got nothing new until he asked, "Have you noticed anything different since your group set up occupancy in the Regent?"

"There's an attic over these dressing rooms, and I've heard someone or something moving around up there. But the door is locked and no one seems to have the key."

"What is stored up there?"

"Nothing. It hasn't been used since there was a revue here in the late 1930s, as far as I know."

"You're certain no one has the key?"

"Ask the stagehands. They wanted to use the area for storage for tools, lumber, that sort of thing."

"We will. Someone must have the key, since you've heard someone up there."

"Or something. You do know this theater is haunted." Marnie looked at each of us in turn with a dramatic pause. When none of us replied, she said, "It's a young woman wearing a pale-colored Victorian dress. She's rumored to be the daughter of a theatrical producer whose father wouldn't let her marry the actor she was in love with. She leaped from the balcony to the floor of the stalls."

"Sounds as if it would be a painful way to die," I commented, my eyes widening as I pictured the disaster.

"I wouldn't care to try it," Marnie said, giving me a small, fellow-sufferer smile.

"How long have you known Si Chapell?" I asked her.

"I've known of Si for many years, first as an actor and then as the editor of *The Stage*. The theater world is a small community and Si is both likeable and flamboyant."

Odd that she made it sound as if she barely knew Si, when he had so recently sent her flowers. Aloud I said, "I didn't know he had been an actor." I said.

Before I could take the conversation any further, the inspector said, "I don't believe what you've heard is a Victorian maiden. I'm going to have the theater searched for the key to the attic storeroom."

The two policemen left, while I sat there with Marnie and Nora. "I want to prove Si is innocent of Lowe's murder," I told them, lowering my voice, "but he won't tell anyone who he was visiting here at the Regent or why. For all I know, he has an alibi for the poisoning."

"He visited me on a few occasions," Marnie said and gave me a smile that must have broken hearts when she was younger.

"Why?"

"We're the same age, give or take a few years. We're old

friends. He wanted my opinion on how the younger actors were doing. And how you were doing." She looked at the ceiling then and shook her head. "And especially how Marshall Lowe was doing."

"Why?"

"I don't know." She widened her blue eyes, looking very innocent, and I suddenly didn't believe a word she told me. I thanked her and walked off to see what I could find.

The stagehands were on the stage itself moving furniture about while arguing and grumbling. I stood and watched them for a few minutes before they noticed me. Gil Baker, the head stagehand, saw me and walked over. "What can I do for you?"

"I've been told you were looking for a key for the attic to store some of your stuff up there," I told him. "Have you found the key yet?"

"No. Have you?"

"No, but the police will be searching for it."

"Why would the police be interested?" Baker looked puzzled.

"Maybe they think there's more poison hidden up there?"

"Unlikely it would be very poisonous now. No one has been up there since Henry VIII."

"Who would be most likely to have the key, if it exists?"

Baker ran a hand over his face. "Old Nick, or one of his equally unreliable predecessors. The owner of the building is probably more likely to still have a copy actually in their possession."

"Who would have the contact details for whoever owns the building?"

"Building manager. You've probably seen him around here. Short, bald, wiry Cockney. Name of Art Jackson. He says he doesn't have the key to the attic. We've already asked him," Baker told me. "And the owner is Harry Morris. He's not likely to be worried about keys, unless they're hotel room keys."

"Where would I find Mr. Jackson?"

"I just saw him go by looking for the producer. Find one, find the other."

"Thank you, Mr. Baker." I gave him a smile and headed for the front of the house.

I found Ian Nelson in a corner of the lobby with a man who met Baker's description of Jackson. As I watched, Nelson opened a door and the two men walked inside. I followed them into a small hallway with dingy offices leading off its linoleum floors and marred paint.

"May I help you, Mrs. Redmond?" Nelson said in a painfully patient voice when he noticed me.

"I was hoping Mr. Jackson could tell me how to get in touch with the owner of the building."

"Why?" the other man barked. While Nelson was dressed for the office, the short, wiry man was dressed for a warehouse. Or a pub. He didn't have a collar attached to his shirt, his sleeves were rolled up, and his braces were visible since he had on neither a waistcoat nor a jacket.

"I thought I'd inquire if anyone had a key to the attic before the police bash in the door."

He folded his arms over his chest. "No."

"It was worth asking before they kick it down."

"No kicking it down."

He could put two words together at one time. "Then you'd better hurry up and find the key." I smiled. "Goodbye."

I went into the lobby and then around the side of the auditorium and up into the wings of the stage. Just as I did, I saw the door to the storeroom by Old Nick's station close.

Had he returned? I walked over to see if he were hiding inside the storeroom.

The door was locked. I looked around. No one was on or behind the stage for the first time since I'd arrived. I knocked loudly, but no one answered the door or made any sound inside that I could hear.

There was nothing for it. I ran back the way I'd come and found Nelson and Jackson arguing about money.

I didn't have time to listen in for the details. "May I have the key for the storeroom near the stage door, please."

"Why?"

"Because someone just went inside and locked the door. We don't want another poisoning, do we?"

Grumbling, Jackson pulled a bunch of keys out of his pocket, took one off the ring, and handed it to me. "Don't lose it."

I raced back to find the door unlocked. I walked in and turned on the light. There was no one there. The dust on the wooden floor and the shelves had been disturbed, but it always was. The rat poison sat on a shelf at eye level. Some parcels were wrapped in brown paper and string, awaiting a member of the cast or crew picking them up and taking them home.

At least they weren't sausages. In this heat, that would stink up the storeroom in record time.

I turned off the light and closed the door. The key in my hand was a large, old-fashioned one. I went down to Marnie's dressing room and found Nora. "Do you know where the entrance to the attic is?" I asked her.

"You have the key?"

"I have a key. I want to see if it might work."

She set down her sewing. "Let's go find out."

We went past the props room and the electricians' room to the far corner of the building where there was a broad, heavy door. I tried the doorknob, but it was locked. Then I tried the key. It opened easily and the door opened without squeaking, as if the hinges had been oiled recently.

Could Jackson really have been unaware that this key opened the attic door? Or had he simply been trying to keep me, or the police, out?

"I have a bad feeling about this," Nora said.

"Is there anyone else around to go up with us?" I asked.

"They're all out for lunch break, including those police oafs."

"Then we have to do this. I'm sure we won't find any ghosts up there."

"Don't be too sure," she told me.

There wasn't a light switch at the bottom of the stairs or a window, so I led the way up the increasingly dark stairwell. "Leave the door open," I called out. By the time I made it to the top of the long flight of stairs, Nora was little more than halfway up.

Another locked door met me at the upper landing, but I felt around in the near darkness until I discovered the key opened that door, too. Once again, the hinges were silent as I swung the door inward.

As I gingerly stepped inside the attic, unable to see the floor or anything else, Nora joined me on the landing. "Is there any light up here?"

I felt around for a light switch without luck, but my hand brushed against something. It was a large battery-powered torch on a table next to the doorway. I picked it up and turned it on. The light shone brightly, telling me the battery was new.

The space covering the area over the dressing rooms and props and electrical cupboards was huge and dusty, but the dust had been disturbed. Long trails of multiple footprints made tracks along the wooden floor, winding between ancient pieces of scenery and furniture clogging the floor space. In a few places, wood angled up toward the vaulted roof. Nothing appeared to have been moved recently and nothing appeared new. Except the torch. And the footprints.

While I was thinking someone must have a key, Nora said, "Marnie will be glad to know it's not ghosts walking around over her head. I'll tell her when she gets back from seeing Si."

Chapter Sixteen

"Wait. What? Marnie's visiting Si at Scotland Yard?" I shone the torch down the stairs as Nora headed for the exit. When she reached the bottom, I yelled, "Leave the door open so I have some light."

She didn't respond, but at least she didn't shut the door.

I turned off the torch, fumbled my way through locking the door, and made my way carefully down the stairs. When I reached the bottom and locked that door, I looked around for Nora but she was nowhere in sight.

No one was on the stage, in the dressing rooms, or backstage except Old Nick, who let out a snore as I passed him. Taking the key, I tiptoed out by the stage door and headed for the *Daily Premier* building.

Fortunately, Sir Henry was in. When I entered his office, I said, "I need a specialized locksmith, and I need information."

"Has that old fool been freed yet?"

"No. Why are you calling Si an old fool?"

"Because he is." Sir Henry sighed and tossed down the pencil he was holding onto his massive desk. "He was originally an actor. And actors are romantics to the core. He's probably protecting someone who doesn't need protecting."

"Marnie Keller."

"How did you find that out?" He gave me a sharp-eyed look.

"She's gone to Scotland Yard to visit him. She's the only one from the theater who has."

"Marnie always was a sweetheart."

Little warning sirens went off in my mind. "How well did you know her?"

"Not as well as Si. That's how I met her. I thought I told you Si was sweet on her."

"You did, but not enough to explain why Si would be sitting in a jail cell for her."

"She didn't do it," Sir Henry scoffed.

"Does he know that? He's been refusing to say anything to the police."

"Still?"

"Yes. And there's something going on in the attic of the Regent. It may just be Old Nick's hiding place, but I'm suspicious because no one seemed to know where the key for it is. Turns out it's the same key as for the cupboard where the rat poison was kept, and I have to return that key to the stage manager. I want to make a duplicate quickly."

"Shouldn't be a problem."

"It's an antique key. Victorian, I guess."

"Talk to Colinswood. He has a contact who's a locksmith specializing in Victorian keys. Don't ask why."

"The same as I shouldn't ask why Si won't say a word

about his whereabouts when Marshall Lowe died?"

"Of course."

"You could be more helpful."

He shook his head. "No, I couldn't. I will call Colinswood to come up here, though."

He called, and then while we waited, he filled me in on what his grandchildren, Johnny and Becca, were doing to drive their mother crazy.

I wasn't too worried, since I knew Esther had a live-in cook and a live-in nursery maid, both refugees who made it out of Germany shortly before the war started. Every time I saw them I was happy for Esther that she had people around her who were such a great help. And that Esther had such a loving heart that she had persuaded her father and me to help her mother's family and other Jewish refugees leave Germany before the war and escape to England.

Mr. Colinswood came in, his clothes smelling of smoke, and heard what I needed. "I'll walk you over there and introduce you. Then I'll leave you to it."

Sir Henry added, "Tell me next time you're going out to see Esther and I'll give you a ride."

Leave it to Sir Henry to still have plenty of petrol while most people had no petrol rations. I agreed and then Mr. Colinswood and I went down in the lift and out onto Fleet Street.

In a few places the street was looking repaired, but for the most part, windows were taped or boarded up and broken bricks were stacked neatly on the sidewalk.

The locksmith's shop was in a boarded-up building in the East End. I would have passed it by if Mr. Colinswood hadn't opened the plank door and walked in. I followed and found to my surprise that the inside was untouched by bomb damage.

Mr. Colinswood and the man inside exchanged a few words, and then I showed him the key, asking for two copies. He took it and walked off through another door. Mr. Colinswood left, leaving me alone.

I wanted to follow him back outside. There was little light in the shop except for a glow around the doorway the man had walked through and a little light coming from between boards in place of the window in front. I wasn't totally certain the building wouldn't collapse on my head, despite the lack of danger signs outside.

However, I trusted Mr. Colinswood. He wouldn't bring me anywhere truly unsafe. I stood there and waited, trying not to swelter in the summer heat. I could have used a cross breeze in the shop, but there was none.

After about a quarter hour, the man returned with three identical keys and then he quoted me a price that hadn't been heard since the Victorian age. I agreed to the bargain, paid him, and left with three keys for the Regent Theatre.

Then I went by the pharmacy where I'd taken Gloria Snelling's makeup to be tested. They were quite definite. Poison ivy.

What a vicious and wide-reaching prank to pull on someone in the theater. Anyone might have used that makeup, and it would have affected anyone touching the contents.

Inspector Dawson and Sergeant Mullins were at the theater when I returned. "I have the stage manager's key," I told them. "It opens both the storeroom by Old Nick's chair and the stairs at the far side of the theater that go to the attic."

I held out one of the copies and the sergeant took it, heading toward the staircase. The inspector and I followed. Once the sergeant unlocked the bottom door, he opened it and turned on a smaller torch that he had been carrying. He led the way up the stairs and then unlocked the door at the top.

"Nora and I came up here earlier today. We stopped in the doorway and tried not to disturb anything," I told the inspector.

"Well, someone has disturbed the dust up here."

"Not us," I said. "It was already looking as if a herd of elephants trooped through here." Even the baking heat hadn't changed by a degree.

The sergeant flashed his torch around the area. "There's quite a bit of junk to climb over." He started out in one direction and the inspector followed. I picked up the larger torch I knew was on the table and turned it on before going in a different direction, sneezing.

Within moments, the inspector was behind me, reaching for the torch. I let him take it and then followed him, studying odd pieces of furniture covered in sheets, stacks of scenery, and bundles wrapped in paper. I touched one. It felt soft and when I tried to write on it with my finger, didn't show any dust. "What is this?"

"Looks as if they are replacement curtains for the front of the stage. These are all old stage props." Inspector Dawson slapped a piece of scenery, sending up a cloud of dust. "Nothing that helps us find a murderer."

We all sneezed.

He turned and went back to the door. "Come along, Sergeant." Turning off the torch, he set it on the table and started back down the stairs. The sergeant lighted our path as he followed us down.

"Yes, someone has been playing the ghost in the attic, frightening Marnie Keller, but I don't think it's our poisoner," Dawson told me. "Let's check that front storeroom where the poison is kept."

I continued to follow them as we crossed behind the stage toward the stage door. Once the sergeant unlocked the door, it was obvious by the bedroll that someone was camping in the storeroom.

"Old Nick?" I asked. The bedroll hadn't been there when I'd looked into the storeroom before going up into the attic.

"That's a good guess. He's supposed to have a key to lock this room up. What better place to bunk down?"

"But is he the killer?" I asked.

"Why would he be?"

"Marshall Lowe found him living here and threatened to throw him out? Housing is difficult to come by since the

Blitz." I should know. I was forced to live with my father. As nice and as large as his house might be, it wasn't big enough for both of us to live there in harmony. We'd already sniped at each other and there'd been plenty of hurt feelings.

"Hardly a reason to kill," the inspector said, tearing me away from my thoughts of just how lethal living conditions could be. "Lock up this room, Sergeant, and put a watch on it. Nothing too obvious, but enough to catch Old Nick when he returns. In the meantime, let's see what Marnie Keller has to say about our prisoner."

The inspector knocked on the door, but this time he was smart enough to wait until someone opened it. It was Nora. "Is Miss Keller available?" he asked.

"Come in, Inspector." Nora held the door open wide and we walked in.

Marnie Keller was wearing a tailored gray business suit with a violet silk blouse and low heels as she sat in front of her dressing table. When she saw us in the mirror she swung around and said, "Welcome. I hear you've found signs of a human presence over our heads and not a ghost."

"That's true. What did you and Si Chapell talk about for ten minutes? The warders said you spoke in code."

"Oh, not in code, Inspector. Whatever makes you say that?" She gave him a demure smile. At least she didn't flutter her eyelashes at him.

"How's the package?"

"What package, Inspector Dawson?"

"The package you and Si Chapell were talking about."

"Oh, that package. Si sent me flowers for opening night."

"Why not just say flowers?"

"Because he doesn't want the other actresses that he doesn't send flowers to knowing that he sends them to some of us. His favorites. Editors of *The Stage* aren't supposed to have favorites." She gave him a smile that could have been seen from the last row of the balcony. I didn't believe a word she said.

"Did Old Nick deliver them to you?" I asked.

"I suppose," she replied in a vague tone. The look she gave me was anything but vague. Had Si been backstage before the opening performance while I was sitting out front?

He was supposed to have watched the opening night of a variety show. He had written a review that we printed. I had thought of that review as his alibi, but perhaps he had faked the review and spent part of the evening in Marnie's dressing room.

Si could have written up what the chairman of the revue told him after the performance. He could have been at the Regent Theatre the entire time and poisoned Marshall Lowe's tea. Marnie wouldn't be much of an alibi for Si since she was onstage a great deal for a character who was supposed to be missing for much of the play.

I decided to let the inspector question Marnie, since any questions I asked would have given away my thoughts.

But I needed to talk to Marnie away from the police. And in the meantime, I needed to talk to the chairman of the revue to learn the truth.

The inspector continued with his questioning, not noticing that I was keeping silent. Perhaps he thought I was amazed at the skill with which he badgered her with useless questions.

"What did you talk about?"

"The weather. He can't see much of the outside world."

"For ten minutes?"

"I've always found the weather is good for at least six or seven minutes."

"And the rest of the time?"

She studied the far wall of the dressing room as if the answer was written there. "Oh, this and that."

"This?"

"And that. Definitely."

"Could you be more specific?"

She thought and then shook her head. "No, I don't think so."

"Miss Keller, what was your purpose for visiting Simon Chapell?"

"He's an old friend."

"Did you see Mr. Chapell on opening night?"

"Oh, dear. I'm not sure."

"How could you not be sure? He's an old friend and it was opening night."

"But darling, there have been so many opening nights in my career. To remember just one of them is difficult." Marnie looked at him wide-eyed, as if she'd had an opening night every week.

In a way, she had. The play had been on tour, opening in a different town nearly every week.

"But this was the most recent opening night. The opening night when your director was poisoned by intermission." The inspector leaned forward to stare directly into Marnie's face. "Poisoned by your lover, Simon Chapell."

Marnie showed how brave she was. She laughed aloud in the inspector's face. "Wrong on two counts, inspector. Si didn't poison anyone, and he's never been my lover. Now, please leave. I have a performance to prepare for."

Inspector Dawson's face turned the color of red wine.

Chapter Seventeen

The police left, having more to do than work on just one murder. I decided it was safe to give Art Jackson, the building manager, his original key back without mentioning that I'd had copies made. I finally found him in the offices to the side of the auditorium with a ledger book and an adding machine.

"Thank you, Mr. Jackson. The police seem to be quite satisfied in the state of your attic."

His bland expression didn't change at the revelation that we'd somehow entered the attic he said there was no key for. "They should be. No one's been up there in years." He took the key from me and put it back on his ring. "If there isn't anything else, I am busy."

"Yes. I'm sorry to have disturbed you." I took the side hallway to the backstage area, hearing the clatter of the adding machine follow me down the hall.

"Livvy. Have you discovered anything?"

I turned to find Gloria Snelling waiting for me at the side of the stage. "Yes. It was poison ivy that was added to your makeup. On the good side, there's nothing to show that you were the target. It would have affected anyone the same way."

"Still, it was a wicked thing to do. Until we find out who did this, we're all in danger. None of us feel safe, Livvy. Please find out who has targeted our play."

"I'll try. In the meantime, keep your eyes open for any more stunts such as that."

Gloria nodded and headed off to her shared dressing room.

I wasn't needed anymore at the Regent and said goodbye to Old Nick on my way out the stage door. "Can't find anybody to hang for Marshall Lowe's death, can ya?" he called after me.

"Not yet. Can you?" I asked, curious to see how he'd respond.

He just tapped the side of his nose.

Then I headed to *The Stage* offices. The new person Sir Henry had sent over to fill in for Si, Mr. Bridges, was making quick work of the advertisements for next week. I'd not met him before, but he apparently knew of me. He looked at me through thick lenses and said, "Sir Henry speaks well of you. You wouldn't have heard of me. I've been stuck in the advertising department of the *Daily Premier* for the past thirty years."

Finding I was no longer needed that day, I decided to check out Si's alibi.

The chairman of the revue Si had reported on that night had the same personality as every other chairman of a revue that I'd ever met. Balding, paunchy, loud, and middle-aged. A man with a long history in the theater. I introduced myself and asked if he'd heard about Si's predicament.

He had and asked me how Marnie was taking it.

I told him she'd been to jail to visit him and was upset.

The man was sympathetic until I asked, "Which one of you wrote the review of the revue?"

Then he became cagey until I assured him I was on Si's side. Then he admitted he had given Si an annotated program for that night after the show.

Si didn't have an alibi.

Then I hurried over to the Green Park Theatre and caught the bookkeeper leaving for the day. I promised him a pint if he'd tell me the old story of the embezzlement involving Ian Nelson and Marshall Lowe.

He didn't know much beyond that there had been an embezzlement. No one was ever charged because their bookkeeping at that time was so sloppy. That was why he was originally hired, to get the theater onto firmer financial footing. However, Lowe and Nelson, either together or separately, were prime candidates for the role of embezzler. They were in the best position to funnel off as much money as they wanted.

Then I went home to find Mrs. Johnson had left us a casserole that only needed baking, so I started the oven and put the covered pan inside. While I waited for my father to return home, I checked the mail. Nothing from Adam that day, which left me feeling flat. Then I trudged upstairs and changed into a housedress and left my feet bare. Once I returned to the kitchen, I set the table.

My father arrived shortly before dinner was due to come out of the oven. He came in the kitchen, said, "You appear to have everything under control," and walked out again.

That was high praise coming from my father. I pulled the dish out on time, spooned it out on two plates, and called for my father. As I was sniffing the dish, the odor was beginning to tie my stomach in knots, so I pushed more of it onto my father's plate. I knew I had to eat something, so I kept enough that he hopefully wouldn't notice how I'd shortchanged myself.

My father came in then, his suit, tie, and waistcoat removed in favor of an old pair of trousers and a light shirt and slippers. He sat down at the wide old kitchen table worn smooth over the years and set his napkin over his lap, waiting to be served.

I served us both and sat, feeling sweat roll down my back. Neither of us spoke until my father said grace, and then silence fell again.

He finished most of his dinner while I was still pushing most of mine around my plate. "Not hungry?" he asked.

"I imagine it's this heat." I tried another spoonful and barely swallowed it. The taste wasn't bad, but the smell was evil.

"Heard from Adam?"

"Not today. Did you want to listen to the radio after dinner?"

"No. I'm going into my study to read my newspaper."

"I'll listen to it if you don't mind."

His response was a cross between a grumble and agreement. I decided to understand him to have agreed.

The silence continued until he finished eating and then he left the room without a word. I did the washing up and then went into the parlor to turn on the radio. After I tuned it into an orchestral program, I opened two of the windows as far as I could and sat in front of one of them, fanning myself with a magazine.

I would have loved a good breeze, but there was hardly enough to flutter the lace curtains. Overheated, I went out to the kitchen for a glass of water and then returned to the slow, plodding music. What I wouldn't give for some rousing music from a bandstand, sitting outside with a breeze threatening to blow my hat off and drinking lemonade.

My father stuck his head into the room. "Good night. The house is locked up."

"Thank you. Good night."

He left, shutting the door, and I heard his slow tread going up the stairs.

Now would be the perfect time to be alone with Adam, listening to the radio, wishing for a breeze, in the silence of the night. I felt my eyes dampen as I thought, "This war has a lot to answer for."

* * *

In the morning, I found I was stuck to the sheets and felt as if I hadn't slept at all. I bathed before I dressed for work. When I went down to the kitchen, I discovered Mrs. Johnson had already arrived and fixed what passed for coffee and toasted some bread. We were out of butter and margarine as well as jam, so I ate mine dry. At least it settled my stomach when I was faced with the smell and taste of bitter coffee.

My father came into the kitchen newly shaved and sat down at his place, expecting his coffee and toast to appear magically, and it always did.

For some reason, his attitude was annoying me that morning. I had to remind myself that this was his house that the Nazis hadn't dared to bomb, while my flat was in rubble and ruin, thanks to the May tenth bombing. I nearly burst into tears again. What was wrong with me?

Mrs. Johnson looked at me, her head to one side, considering. "Is something wrong, Livvy?"

"I'm upset and grumpy. Must be this heat wave, Mrs. Johnson."

"I don't think I slept a wink all night long," she told me. "Not a breeze anywhere. And we still have August to get through."

"Oh, don't remind me," I grumbled. "And Adam complains that it's cold where he is and he wishes they could turn on the heat."

"All he has to do is put on more clothes. It's not as if we can take some of ours off."

"Oh, please don't, Mrs. Johnson," my father said with complete seriousness from behind his newspaper.

I managed to stop a giggle in time.

"As if, Sir Ronald. As if. Does Adam say when he'll be

down here again?" she asked.

"Not a word. I miss him terribly," I added, blinking away tears.

"This war hasn't been easy on you, but don't worry, it will get better. Adam will be here soon, if only on leave. Want more coffee?"

"No, thank you."

Mrs. Johnson put my dirty dishes in the sink, and I gathered up my things for another day of work.

"I'll see you tonight?" I asked my father.

"I'm going to a dinner at my club tonight. I won't be home until late. No need for you to cook dinner for us, Mrs. Johnson."

Mrs. Johnson looked at me, eyebrows raised.

"If you could leave me an egg and some soup or broth, I can fend for myself quite well, Mrs. Johnson," I told her with a smile.

"I will, and some bread. The leftover loaf will do well for toast in the morning."

"It sounds as if it will be a feast. Thank you." I headed off to the offices of *The Stage* in a cheerier frame of mind.

Mr. Bridges was already in the office when I arrived wilting from the growing heat in the Underground and on the streets.

"How are you getting on?" I asked.

"I have the adverts all arranged for next week's paper. It just needs your column, the news, and a couple of reviews."

"Speaking of reviews, Mr. Bridges, have you ever wanted

to write one? Do you care for musical and comedy revues?" Those were Si's specialties, and doing those reviews would have been a tight squeeze for me.

You would have thought I'd offered him the crown jewels. His narrow face was split by a smile before he managed to say, "But would it be allowed?"

"Of course. The chairman of the revue you write up for next week's paper will help you with names, song titles—he may write the whole thing for you if you let him. Just tell him you're from *The Stage* replacing Si Chapell until the police release him."

"How much will it cost me?"

"Tell the girl at the box office you're from *The Stage* and to call the chairman. You get in for free and if you stick around after the show, you'll get all you need for the review and also get to meet some of the performers. Just be polite and praise everyone equally. Or as equally as you can."

"While you?" He looked a little skeptical.

"Write up the column and the play review. Shakespeare in the Southwark Park this week."

"Better you than me." He made a face at the word "Shakespeare."

"In that case, Mr. Bridges, we should get along fabulously."

In the end, I took him to the theater we needed to review that week and introduced him to the chairman of the revue. I picked up a couple of details for my column and Mr. Bridges was all set to spend the afternoon watching a new revue with plenty of comedy, music, and dancing girls. After we left, I marched Mr. Bridges through the heat to another revue theater where they were in rehearsals. I set my colleague up with the chairman to review his production several nights later on opening night and picked up a couple more bits for my column that week.

Then I sent Mr. Bridges on his way back to the office and I went down to Scotland Yard and asked to see Si Chapell. The warder in the basement area told me he'd been before a magistrate and was to be held over for trial at HMP Pentonville. Maybe he took pity on me or maybe he knew how Pentonville appeared to outsiders, but he told me there was an hour allowed for visitors starting at eleven.

I looked at my watch and knew I had to hurry.

Taking the Piccadilly Line to the Caledonian Road station, I walked in the heat to the entrance to the prison. I arrived a little after eleven at the entrance to the Victorian gothic structure and was shown to a small room on the ground floor. A few minutes later, Si was led in.

"I am so glad to see you," he said.

"When did they bring you out here?"

"Last night after I saw the inside of the magistrate's court. Not any place I'd want to see again. They made their suppositions sound as if they were facts and convinced the magistrate that no one else could have killed Marshall Lowe." He leaned forward over the table that sat between us. "You've got to get me out of here. It's horrible in here. Killers and thieves and black-market gangsters."

He was wearing a prison uniform, a dull, ill-fitting outfit so unlike his brightly colored waistcoat and tie. He looked pale and he shivered, although I thought the cool felt nice and refreshing inside the thick stone walls after battling the heat outside. Unfortunately, it also held in decades of smells I didn't want to identify in case my stomach couldn't handle the stench.

"What you need is a solicitor to get you out," I told him.

"What solicitor? I don't know any solicitors."

"I'll ask Sir Henry. He must know some."

"Is he keeping *The Stage* going?" That was always Si's first concern.

"Yes. He has two of us working there now."

"Good. Thank you."

I leaned forward. "Now, what really happened?"

"Nothing."

"Nonsense. If you're going to give me answers such as those, you deserve to hang. What happened?"

He lowered his voice to a whisper. "I went to see Marnie. Just to wish her a good opening night. I brought her some flowers."

"And?"

"What do you mean 'and?'" He leaned back.

"Did you leave her dressing room at any time?"

"Of course. I wasn't there long. I had left by the opening curtain." Si wore an expression of annoyance mixed with anger.

"Did anyone walk you in or out? See you while you

walked to and from her dressing room?"

"No. I didn't know I'd need an alibi, did I?"

"Si, what did they say to have the court hold you over for trial?"

"I'd been there that night. I had no reason to be there, except to poison Lowe. That I hated him. That I refused to say anything."

"I've heard you'd had trouble with Marshall Lowe in the past." If Si wasn't willing to tell me anything, I doubted I could help him.

"All in the past, Livvy. If anything, he did me a favor. He pointed out I wasn't much of an actor, something my friends wouldn't do. That led, eventually, to *The Stage*."

"And you haven't had anything else to do with Marshall Lowe until this past week?"

Si held empty hands out to me. "I've written reviews of his plays any number of times over the years. Most of them were favorable. And I saw him each time, if only to nod to or say hello."

"What about Marnie?"

"What about her? The same as most of Britain, I worship at that woman's feet. She's arguably our best comic actress."

"Has it ever been more than that?" I asked him.

"No. Of course not. She flirts with me a little as she does with all her admirers, but that's all."

"What about when you were both young? Was it just a flirtation between the two of you then?"

"That's all it's ever been." Si stood up and walked toward

the door. "I'm tired of hearing this nonsense from you and the police. Frankly, it's insulting. Good day, Livvy." A guard opened the door and he strode out.

I rose slowly from my seat. Somebody needed to tell me the truth about Si's relationship with Marnie, or I wouldn't get anywhere.

Si didn't deserve to hang, but if we couldn't find the guilty party and Si wasn't honest with someone, he was going to die.

Chapter Eighteen

I left HMP Pentonville and took the Tube back to the west end of London. I needed to find out how Marnie really felt about Si and how their relationship had been many years ago. But first I found I was hungry and stopped at one of the British Restaurants that had popped up to serve the vast numbers of workers now that housewives had gone out to work. The vegetable marrows and beans were well cooked and teamed with some pork flavor, if not actual pork, and I paired it with a roll.

A halfway satisfying meal and off the ration, to make up for the skimpy dinner I would have that night. The restaurant was busy, since so many women had gone to work in offices and factories and were no longer available to cook their own and their family's meals.

Fortunately, when I arrived at the Regent after lunch, Marnie was in her dressing room preparing for a matinee. "I've got bad news," I told her. "The police have charged Si Chapell with Marshall Lowe's murder. He's been transferred to Pentonville and he's terrified."

Marnie paled. "They can't do that."

"They did. I've just seen him there. Apparently, it's a

pretty rough jail and he wants out."

"Has he seen a solicitor?"

"I don't think so. I asked him and he said he doesn't know any."

She picked up a piece of paper and frantically began to scribble a note. When she finished, she handed it to Nora without showing it to me. "Take it to Holland and Smythe and then come right back. I'll need you between performances." Then she turned her brilliant smile on me. "Livvy will be my dresser for the matinee."

"Wouldn't it be better if I took it to the solicitor's office?" I asked, having seen she'd not sealed up the note.

"No. This will be a good experience for you."

Nora went off looking doubtful. Whether she already knew what was going on or could be trusted not to peek at the paper, I didn't know, but this would give me a chance to question Marnie.

"When did Si leave your dressing room the night of the murder?"

She paused in putting on her stage makeup. "Just a few minutes after the start of the play."

"Who saw him leave?"

"No one that I know of. Except Nora."

"What motive do the police have for Si murdering Marshall Lowe? You, out of everyone, should know." I watched her as she put on her makeup in silence. "No one can help Si until we know that."

She sighed, her shoulders slumping. "For a brief period,

Marshall Lowe was my husband. He could be a beastly man to everyone, but he was worse to his wives and lovers." She turned away from her mirror to face me. "That's why it's ridiculous that the police think Si killed him. He was never married to Marshall."

I blinked. I hadn't thought of that angle. "Was he Marshall's lover?"

She shook her head and looked annoyed. "Neither man was so inclined."

"Then why are the police fixated on Si?"

"Because he originally lied and said he wasn't here at all. A silly mistake. Now, help me into my dress for the first act."

After she stepped out of her dressing gown with its few marks of greasepaint, I lifted her dress over her head. As I did, I said, "There's more to it than that. Whatever his secret is, it involves you, Marnie. You're the reason he's stuck in Pentonville."

She expertly slid her arms through the sleeves as I adjusted the frock. Then she turned for me to button her up. I did and said, "What's the big secret, Marnie? Si's locked away in prison awaiting trial for murder, for which he'll be hanged. Is the secret that important?"

"Wish me a broken leg," Marnie said as she headed out of her dressing room.

"The same as Wanda Thomas?" I asked, but I don't think she heard me.

I followed, more slowly, and watched the first scenes. Marnie was in her usual comedic form, and the audience was with her, laughing at her jokes and applauding enthusiastically when she walked offstage.

"Has Nora returned?" she asked when she saw me.

"I don't know. I've been watching you."

Marnie let the way to her dressing room, beaming when she saw Nora sitting in her usual spot sewing.

Nora leaped up, saying, "Let me straighten your frock."

Marnie stopped in the center of the room to allow Nora to make trivial tweaks here and there. "What did the solicitors say?"

"They'll be out to see him in the morning."

"Thank goodness. And they'll talk to Scotland Yard about the charges?"

"I think it's His Majesty's Prosecution Service, but whoever they need to talk to about dropping charges, they will." Nora put her hands on Marnie's shoulders. "Si will have to tell them the truth."

"He's a writer. He'll think of something."

"The solicitors will have to know."

"Solicitor-client privilege. It won't have to go any further."

"It will. Just the way Marshall wanted."

I was aware of two things. Marshall Lowe wanted something to come out that Marnie and Si wanted kept quiet, giving them a motive. And Nora called the director "Marshall." Not "Mr. Lowe."

If Nora knew him that well, it had to go back to when Marnie was married to the director. But why did that need to be a secret?

So Marshall Lowe, Nora, Marnie, and Si all knew the secret. Why wouldn't they tell me? I had promised not to tell anyone. Sir Henry must have told Si I had a blameless record. The police couldn't use anything I said because it would be hearsay, so I wouldn't be required to tell them.

This secret had to be much bigger than anything I had dreamed up.

* * *

Nora made it clear by her stares that I was no longer needed at the Regent, and while Marnie was kinder about it, she also let me know I'd worn out my welcome.

I looked around, making sure Detective Inspector Dawson and Sergeant Mullins weren't in the theater, and then I left for the open-air Shakespeare stage south of the river in Southwark Park.

It was a warm afternoon with few clouds in the sky. Crowds were pouring into the area from all directions when I arrived, appearing to be in a good mood and expecting a good show to divert them from the fears and hardships we all faced.

Loudspeakers were set up along the edge of the park so that the latecomers, who wouldn't be able to see the action on the stage, could still hear the actors.

I found the producer and introduced myself before I was shown to a spot where I could watch and write up my review for *The Stage.* By the time the play began, I was melting and my skin felt as if it was on fire. The heat didn't seem to bother the audience. They were ready to laugh.

That week's performance was *Twelfth Night*, a crowd pleaser with a universal appeal even more absorbing than the war that surrounded us and a good deal more pleasurable. Whoever chose that one of Shakespeare's plays for the second set of performances in the park had done well. Despite having to stand in the heat outside the walls, the overflow audience was as drawn in as the crowd near me and the stage.

Afterward, I moved to near the stage where the actors were talking to critics and sponsors. Whenever I said I was from *The Stage,* the actors around me immediately asked how Si was holding up.

The only thing I felt I could say was he was proclaiming his innocence and he had finally agreed to a solicitor. They all wished him well.

An older actor playing a small part said in a low voice, "That was never going to end well."

"What wasn't?" I asked him.

"I shouldn't gossip." He turned to walk away.

I rushed to block his way and said, "I wish you would. Nobody can help Si if somebody doesn't talk."

"Fine." He gestured me a little farther from the group. "This goes back to when Si was still acting. He had a small part in a play where Marnie Keller...do you know her?"

"Yes."

"She had the role of the ingenue and Marshall Lowe was directing. They were married and—" He raised his eyebrows.

"I'd heard Marnie and Lowe were married." There was no surprise in my tone, but I needed to know more because Marnie acted as if no one knew about their long-ago liaison. "Do you know what went wrong?"

"Of course. They hadn't been married long and from the way Si was hanging around Marnie, that marriage wasn't going to last."

"What happened?"

"What do you think happened? Marnie and Lowe fought in the theater one day, she was in tears, Si intervened, he and Lowe came to blows, and Si was thrown out of the play. He never worked as an actor again. Lowe had him banned from the London theaters. Marnie and Lowe divorced. Once the play's run ended, Marnie couldn't get a job in the theater for a full year until somebody stood up to Lowe. She was too good an actress to be left on the shelf for so long."

"Do the police know about this? Is this why Si was arrested for poisoning Marshall Lowe?" I asked.

"My dear child, how would I know what the police are thinking?" He turned away, but I had one more question before I'd let him go.

I put a hand on his arm to stop him. "Did Lowe or Marnie ever marry again?"

"Neither one. And neither did Si. And that is absolutely my last word on the subject." He walked off and I stood there for a minute, thinking about what I'd just heard.

Then I hurried to the Regent Theatre where the second performance of the day would be wrapping up.

I headed straight for the stage door, hoping they hadn't replaced Old Nick in my absence. They hadn't, but there was a police constable guarding the entrance. Old Nick was sitting in his ratty chair watching the action around him.

"What's happened?" I asked.

"You can't go in," the constable said, not moving a muscle in the doorway.

"Why? What has happened since this afternoon's performance?"

"You can't go in," he repeated.

"Then may I speak to Detective Inspector Dawson or Sergeant Mullins?"

"They're busy."

"How do you know if you don't ask them?"

At that moment, a bicycle delivery man rode up with a big bouquet of flowers. "These are for Miss Carroll," he said and pushed them into the policeman's chest so that he had to grab them.

I took the opportunity and hurried inside. I could hear the last scene being performed onstage so I hurried to Marnie's dressing room. Nora was in her usual place, sewing.

"I've heard twice now that Marnie and Marshall Lowe were married. Why is that such a big secret?"

She glanced up at me and then looked back at the cloth in her hands. "That was a long time ago."

"How long ago?"

"Thirty years, thirty-two. Something near that." She shrugged.

"Before the Great War?"

"That's about right."

"Is it true Si Chapell broke up their marriage?"

"No. Don't be daft, child. Marshall Lowe never had any trouble breaking up any relationship he had with anyone."

I knew Nora was devoted to Marnie, and I suspected she would always take Marnie's side. "Lowe was cruel to Marnie, wasn't he?"

"Cruel, brutal, vicious. But he always made sure to hit her where it didn't show."

"Why did she stay with him?"

"She didn't. They were married less than two years. And before the Great War, getting a divorce that quickly took some doing."

"The only way I can think of back then to get a divorce was if… Golly, he charged Marnie with adultery." I was shocked. And if I was, the theater-going public would be more so. Marnie was such a sweet, joyful creature.

Nora and I held a staring contest for at least a minute before she lowered her head and nodded. "The publicity would have been horrible if the news got out. And if you think it would be bad now, think how things were before the Great War. Divorce was scandalous. Lowe threatened to reveal it any time he wanted Marnie to do something or not do something. He kept her off the stage for a year or more with his threats until…"

"Until what?"

"Until a producer wanted Marnie in a production. This

was a big producer, a man with serious clout during the Great War, and he could have seriously hurt Marshall's career. He had to give in at the end and let Marnie go back to work."

"He beat her, he divorced her, he tried to end her career. What an odious man." I could see why no one shed a tear over his passing.

"Nora, have you been entertaining our young friend with tales of my past indiscretions?" Marnie came in, her face flushed from the applause and her curtain calls.

"Someone told her. I just told her from your point of view."

"Not the police, I hope."

"I don't know what they know. But I don't see how this old story has any bearing on what Si might or might not do today." I looked to Marnie to explain this to me.

She shook her head. "I was in love with Si, and he with me. But the divorce, the trashing of both our careers, ruined what love there was between us. But he would never have killed Marshall over something that happened over thirty years ago."

"What happened over thirty years ago?" Inspector Dawson stood in the doorway.

Chapter Nineteen

"A great deal more than what has occurred so far in your murder investigation," Marnie told him. "Now, if you don't mind, I would appreciate being able to get changed and go home before the blackout leaves us all wandering around in the dark."

"We'll talk about this tomorrow. Be at Scotland Yard tomorrow at nine. And we will expect some honest answers if you don't want to find yourself in a jail cell." The policeman disappeared from the doorway.

"I have a long distance to travel to get home. I'll see you tomorrow," I told Marnie. "And thank you for your honesty."

I left by the stage door and passed the policeman who was ignoring anyone not trying to get into the theater. Someone who resembled Old Nick was ahead of me in the alley but had disappeared by the time I reached the street.

The last twilight was fading as I reached my father's street. The evening was warm, but the days were starting to shorten, if only by a few minutes. I didn't want to think about the onset of darkness and rain when autumn finally settled in.

At least I wouldn't be roasting as I had this summer.

When I was in school, summer holidays were my favorite part of the year, either traveling with my father or staying in London with Esther. When had I become so old that summer was no better than autumn?

* * *

I met my father at the breakfast table the next morning. I had coffee and dry toast while my father only had coffee, proclaiming anything else to be an abomination against what breakfast should be.

Mrs. Johnson arrived and immediately checked the pantry to see I'd eaten the egg and the broth she'd left me the night before. "That's hardly a filling dinner," she told me.

"It's too hot for proper meals at night. I was grateful for the egg and the soup broth. It was just right."

"I ate at the club," my father said. "It's the first fully satisfying meal I've had since I ate at the Savoy. I have to get away from rationing every once in a while."

"We all do," I grumbled and immediately regretted my lack of manners. "I may agree with you in the autumn when it comes to eating dinner. Right now, it's too hot to think about eating," I told him.

"Are you certain you're all right?" Mrs. Johnson asked me.

"I'm fine. Don't worry," I told her. "When the seasons change, I'll be able to eat."

"Did you hear from Adam yesterday?" my father asked.

"Yes. He's well and it was raining when he wrote. No word on when his next visit would be." Those words always depressed me. I wanted to spend more time with my husband, but since he was an army officer and we had a war going on all around us, my wishes were sitting on the back burner at the Ministry of Defense.

My father left for work earlier than I did that morning, which was all right with me, and on a Saturday, which meant things were heating up in the Foreign Ministry. This gave me time to think. I felt certain Si hadn't killed Marshall Lowe, but who had? I couldn't see any of the stage crew killing him. Lowe simply didn't have enough to do with any of them, and I'd been told he couldn't fire them.

It had to be an actor. But which one?

With that determination behind me, I went to *The Stage* office in Bush House. Mr. Bridges was there ahead of me again, finishing up as much as he could of the mockup of this coming week's issue.

I finished my write-up of *Twelfth Night*, giving lavish praise to the actors, and helped Mr. Bridges set up the pages of this week's edition. Once we were certain this much of the issue was error-free, Mr. Bridges started on the adverts and personal notices that would go in the next week's issue.

After I left the newspaper office, I was free for the rest of the day. I decided my first place to stop was at Scotland Yard.

I was escorted to Inspector Dawson's office, where I found him poring over reports. "Come in and shut the door," he told me.

"Have you found the real killer?" I asked.

"I found out what Chapell has been hiding."

"Oh?" I wondered who squealed about the love triangle of Marshall Lowe, Marnie Keller, and Simon Chapell.

"Chapell's been stuck on the margins, watching as Lowe has gone on to ever bigger successes, while he has to report on the other man's triumphs. Lowe fired him, trashed his reputation as an actor, and Chapell had no way to settle the score. Then the woman who came between them, Marnie Keller, comes back to London starring in a Marshall Lowe production. Chapell is still in love with her, and he sees his old nemesis and the love of his life laughing and succeeding together. It's too much. He finds the rat poison, he knows which teacup is Lowe's, and the rest you can figure out."

"Have you told this to Mr. Chapell?"

"Yes." He couldn't meet my gaze.

"And?" I raised my eyebrows. I could picture the scene in my mind.

"He admits nothing."

"He probably laughed at you." It was hard for me not to laugh, too.

Dawson growled as he tossed down a report and leaned back in his chair. "You're not far off the mark," he admitted.

"I went to see Shakespeare performed in Southwark Park yesterday. Afterward, all the actors told me to wish Si well. No one had a good thing to say about Lowe. Si is a very popular man with the power to help people through the press. He has a job that he enjoys and that he is good at. He is every bit as successful as Lowe was."

"That doesn't make him innocent."

Dawson, I decided, was just being stubborn because he had no other suspects. "Just don't lose sight of some other possibilities. Someone has been up in the attics, and it's not on theater business. Old Nick has disappeared and reappeared from his job as gatekeeper of the stage door so many times no one is ever quite certain where he is. When he was at his seat, he was well-positioned to see who took the rat poison and put it in Lowe's mug."

"I'm surprised you haven't mentioned Bud Cosby."

I stopped to think about him in relation to the attics and the poison. Then I realized what Dawson meant. "Because he had a better idea of what to do with Lowe's play, whether or not it was stolen and heavily revised, and he couldn't show how much better his ideas were until Lowe was out of the way. More important, have you found out if Philip Bernard, the author of the play, has any living relatives?"

"The grandmother died in an asylum, which was the best place for her. She murdered Bernard's mother, and his uncle hanged for the crime. He was an only child. Father was out of the picture—"

"Dead?"

"Possibly. Grandfather was dead, later found chopped up under the stairs—"

"Good heavens." That poor child. No wonder Philip Bernard had been unhinged.

"Uncle was apparently a loner. If there was any other family, we haven't found them."

"Neighbors?"

"Kept their distance."

I couldn't say I blamed them. I'd have been in hiding.

"As long as you're here, go back to the Regent with me while we go through the cupboards and the attics. Mullins!" He stood and I followed him out of his office to see the sergeant hurry down the hallway toward us. "We're going back to search the cupboards and attics again to see if we missed anything."

"You think Chapell hid something in one of them?" Mullins asked.

"The murder might have been necessary to hide another crime," Dawson replied. He led the way out of the building and then we began to walk in the heat. There was a breeze, but all it did was blow around the dust from the bomb sites. The construction work on those sites where it was deemed necessary despite fear of continuing bombing added to the dust.

Mullins and I both sneezed. Inspector Dawson shook his head and marched on.

"Did you talk to Marnie Keller this morning?" I asked.

"Yes, but it wasn't completely successful. There's still more there between her and Chapell," Dawson said. "I'm sure of it."

We entered the stage door after the inspector spoke to the constable on duty. There was no sign of Old Nick. I opened up the storeroom near the stage door, but there hadn't been any visible differences from our last look in there.

"What are you doing with an extra key to the storerooms?" Dawson asked me.

I froze. How could I have been so careless? "I don't remember," I lied. I couldn't see explaining to the police that I'd had it made when only one key was locatable.

He eyed me narrowly, but said nothing.

I was very glad the inspector didn't ask me to hand it over. I'd already given the police one key while we were investigating Lowe's murder. That was all I was giving them. I trailed the two policemen upstairs to the attics.

When we reached the bottom door to the stairway, the inspector pulled out the key I'd given him and unlocked the door before switching on his torch. I could have kicked myself. He'd had it all along. I followed the two policemen up the stairs and grabbed the torch by the door.

The dust had been disturbed on the floor since we'd been up there last, making me sneeze again. I followed the widest path until it ended by two short piles of brown paper-wrapped packages. "There's been a lot of activity right here," I called out to the policemen who were searching another trail in the dust.

"Bolts of new fabric here. Suit fabric. Shirt fabric," Dawson said as he walked over to where I waited. He checked some of the packages around me. "Bolts of dress fabric here. I think we've found the hiding place for a black-market operation."

"Could Marshall Lowe have found out about it and been

killed to keep their secret safe?" I asked.

"It's possible." He sounded grudging, but I'd take it.

"Then Si Chapell is not the only suspect."

Inspector Dawson looked at me and shook his head. "This does change things, especially as it appears to be a large-scale operation."

"Will you release Si from custody?"

"Possibly. Depends on what other suspects we turn up."

That was an improvement.

"Let's see if there's anything else up here," Dawson said and walked back to another trail that branched off from the one I had followed. I tried to step in his dustless footprints around a corner and behind more scenery. From there we found more packages of fabric.

"We haven't covered all of the theater yet, have we?" I asked.

"Is there any hiding place left?" Dawson asked.

"We'll have to ask the building manager, Art Jackson," I replied. I'd have done it anyway, but it seemed more prudent to get an inspector to ask.

As they shone their torches around, we could see nothing else had been disturbed in the attics. I couldn't imagine anyone wanting to be up there in this heat. Eventually, we went downstairs and found Jackson in the backstage area where it was a degree or two less hot, although still not cool, but certainly much less dusty.

Jackson screwed up his face in thought when the inspector asked him, "Have you been in the cellars?"

"Where is the way leading down?" Dawson asked, looking around him.

Jackson led us to a door I hadn't checked out before and, as the policemen turned their torches back on, started down a long wooden stairwell to a rough cement floor. The area appeared empty, but there were noises echoing around us.

The manager saw me looking around in confusion. "Over that way is one of the underground rivers that flows into the Thames. You can hear the water running. Take that stairwell down and follow the trail that way to find it. In that direction is the Tube. Go that way and there's a ladder down to the line. Piccadilly. You can listen to the trains as they roll past."

Mullins went behind the stairway into the shadows and said, "Look here, sir."

While there was no one there currently, the bedroll and sack holding clothing showed someone, a man, was living there. "Are these Old Nick's things?" Dawson asked, holding up a shirt and waistcoat.

They were working-class clothes, but I said, "No. Old Nick is smaller than whoever wears these things. One of the electricians, or stagehands maybe, who've been bombed out of their home?"

"Then where is Old Nick?"

"Think he's done a runner, sir?" Mullins asked.

"I think this must have been Old Nick's hidey-hole where he said he hid during the Blitz. And once down here, he found that he could go in half a dozen different directions," I told Dawson. "But I don't think he's in hiding. When we go back up to the theater, he'll probably be back in his chair."

Unlike the attic where you could feel the heat simmer off the roof, in the basement most people would have needed a jacket. I was finally comfortable.

"There's nothing for us to see down here," the inspector said. "Let's go back upstairs." But first, instead of doing that, he rounded on the building manager. "Who's living in your cellar?"

"What?"

"It's a simple question."

"No one. Nobody's living in the cellar." Jackson looked around him in panic, with wide eyes and a slack jaw. "It's too cold."

"Would you say it's cold down here?"

"Y-yes."

"Then why are you sweating?"

"Maybe he's afraid you've discovered the black-market goods in the attic," I suggested.

All three men turned to stare at me. Apparently, that wasn't what I was supposed to say.

"That's not mine," Jackson protested, holding his hands up.

"Then whose is it? You're not handing out keys to the attic as if they were a door prize. Who did you give a key to?"

"You." There was a definite sneer on his face as he looked at me.

"That won't wash," I said. "We have evidence the black-market goods were up there before I ever got a key from you."

"Ha. What evidence?"

"The trails where the dust was rubbed away by footsteps. Trails that lead right to the black-market goods." I gave him a satisfied smile.

"Doesn't mean I had anything to do with it."

"But you're the keeper of the keys."

"That was Old Nick. That is his job."

"Who has conveniently disappeared. Again."

"He hasn't disappeared, I saw him a few minutes ago when he said he'd take his lunch break before we get busy," Jackson said.

"Mullins, get the constable on the door to bring some men in to take photos of the contraband for a warrant and then wait at the bottom of the staircase. Jackson, you and I are going to have a talk in your office. Mrs. Redmond, you are no longer needed." The inspector took Jackson by the arm and started up the stairs, leaving me to stay in the cellar or go up to the stage on my own.

I'd been dismissed.

Chapter Twenty

I watched them disappear up the staircase while I fumed. I did not enjoy being dismissed. At least the presence of another suspect made it more likely Si Chapell would be released.

Fortunately, Inspector Dawson had left me with a torch that allowed me to search the bedroll and sack of clothes. The bedroll offered up nothing in the way of clues, but inside the waterproof cloth bag of clothing I found a photo buried at the bottom. It was dog-eared and bent, but it was clearly a photograph of a dark-haired mother with two children, an older sister and younger brother, both with fair hair. The clothing and hair-styles showed it was an old photo taken at a studio, probably during the 1920s.

I flipped it over. On the back was written in a printed hand, "Mum, Carol, and me." I made a note in my book of any details that might be helpful and then put everything back the way I'd found it.

Once I climbed up to the stage level, I went looking for Marnie. She and her dresser, Nora, were in her dressing room, starting the process of getting her ready for that night's performance.

"The police have another theory about Marshall Lowe's death and they've taken Art Jackson to his office to answer some questions about the black-market goods stored here," I told them. "This may be enough to get Si released."

"Thank goodness," Marnie said. "Give me a hand with my face, Nora. I'm so excited Si may get out soon I can't keep my fingers still."

"Art Jackson was running a black market out of here?" Nora said as she picked up a pot of face paint. "What is he selling?"

"Fabric."

"He'd never." Nora's tone was scoffing. "He wouldn't think of it. He can run a building, but not a business. They don't let him near the box office receipts. Ian Nelson manages all the money, box office and payroll, the advertising, and pays the rent directly to the man who owns the building."

"Then why did I see Jackson going over the ledgers in the office?" I asked. "With an adding machine."

"Really? I'm very surprised. Jackson has told me before that he can't add up the receipts." Nora looked puzzled.

"And yet he was," I told her.

"Hmm."

"So, who would be running a black-market operation out of here?" I was certain Nora would have a better idea than I would.

"I don't know. Leave it with me." Nora turned her concentration to Marnie's face.

"Also, where does Old Nick keep disappearing to? I'm sure he used the cellars for his own private bomb shelter, but I think the clothes down there now are someone else's. Old Nick seems to disappear more often than your character in the play, Marnie."

"Haven't you figured it out by now?" Marnie asked without moving her lips as Nora applied a cream. "He's done time for crimes of violence before, and he figures another violent act, where he works, is going to have him put away again. Or hanged. Whenever the police come around the backstage area, Old Nick takes off for an hour."

"I see him as I walk in the doorway, but when I return a few minutes later, he's gone."

"One of the stagehands thought he saw Old Nick in their local a day or two ago," Marnie said with a big smile. "I think that might be where he bides his time. I'll be glad when he's back doing his job."

"Why would you miss that crazy old lay-about?" Nora asked, focused on Marnie's makeup.

"He's been here forever. He does his job," Marnie replied. "And he was nice to that playwright, Philip Bernard. He was the only one who was. If the rest of us had treated that young man the way Old Nick did, maybe he wouldn't have killed himself."

"He was mad. Drugs or something," Nora said. "Nothing you or anyone else could have done for him."

"I wonder if insanity ran in his family. His grandmother killed a couple of people, didn't she?" I sat down on the chair near the door.

"That home must have been a horrible place for a child to grow up. Why didn't his mother leave and take him with her? It might have made a happier ending that way," Nora replied. She patted Marnie's face with powder.

"Oh, Nora," Marnie said, her eyes shut to keep out any stray makeup, "many women aren't as determined as you or I."

"Neither of us has had the time or place to be anything but determined and to protect ourselves and our loved ones. What do you think?" Nora added as she studied the finished makeup on Marnie's face.

Marnie opened her eyes and looked in the mirror. She took a deep breath and blinked as if Nora's words had affected her before she put on a bright smile and said, "Perfect. Thank you. What are you going to do now to help free Si Chapell?"

I had been trying to picture Nora as a mother and was failing. "That solicitor you talked to will have an easier time getting Si released now that there is a whole group of possible killers among the black-market thieves."

"To protect their secret if Marshall had figured out what they were doing?" Nora asked. "Yes, that makes sense."

"Are you going to stay and watch today's performance?" Marnie asked me.

Why not? I didn't want to spend time at home with my father. Adam wasn't in town. Most of my friends were out of London. Then I remembered.

"*Lady, Behave* is opening tonight at His Majesty's. I have to cover it for the paper next week."

"Oh, that new musical comedy," Marnie said with a note of disdain in her voice. "Come back here afterward—maybe we'll be able to tell you if Si has been released by then. And whether we agreed with your reviews this week." She gave me a wide smile. It reminded me of a crocodile.

"How could I resist the chance to hear my work be shredded item by item?"

"Good. We'll see you back here as quick as you can."

"The first thing I'm going to do is get lunch." With the heat later on in the day, lunch was the only meal I enjoyed. What with following the police around, it would be a late lunch that day.

I dined on tea and vegetables roasted with a hint of meat and a roll without butter and then went over to introduce myself to the producer of *Lady, Behave*. It was the first time I'd been in His Majesty's Theatre, grandiose on the outside, a narrow, paneled entrance inside, and then the magnificent dark red plush seats. I was given a program to help with my review, chatted with the nervous producer and slightly panicked director, and then was left on my own in the cavernous auditorium. Without other bodies in there, it was quite cool by comparison.

The auditorium was warm by the time the performance began and the crowd had arrived and settled in. The play was fun, there were a lot of laughs, and a few good tunes rang in my ears by the time it finished. I had scribbled notes on my program, so I hurried away to return to the Regent.

There was no policeman on the stage door, so I went in that way and said hello to Old Nick. I could hear Marnie Keller and Bud Cosby on stage, so I was pretty sure they were halfway through the last act after intermission. What surprised me was seeing Inspector Dawson and Sergeant Mullins backstage watching the youngest stagehand.

The young man kept looking over his shoulder at the policemen. When the scene ended, Gil Baker, the head stagehand, had to hiss a few words at his helper to put him in motion. They worked to pull the scenery up into the rafters and then tied it off. Then they walked onto the stage to help the others move furniture around for the next scene.

Less than thirty seconds later, all four stagehands came off the stage on the side opposite where they'd walked on. The young man, realizing the police were still watching the other side of the stage, tried to slip away.

I touched Dawson's sleeve and pointed, setting him and the sergeant into motion. I followed at a subdued pace, and by the time I reached the door to the upstairs stairway, the young man was already on the floor and cuffed.

"Hey, what are you doing?" Gil Baker asked in a low but powerful voice. "We're in the middle of a play."

"He has to leave early," Dawson said, pulling the young man upright and starting toward the stage door on the far side of the backstage area. He swung around to face me and added, "Not you this time."

I followed discreetly until I heard him say, "We need

transport to the Yard."

Then I turned back to stand by Baker and said, "We'll talk after the performance."

He nodded, still looking worried.

As soon as the play ended, I was congratulating Marnie when Gil Baker came up to me. "Why did they take Joe Landry away in handcuffs?"

"I'm not sure if they think he killed Marshall Lowe, was running the black market out of here, or both."

"Are you joking? That boy couldn't organize tea, much less commit murder or fence black market goods." Baker shook his head. "He's useless, but that's not a crime. It's the only one he's guilty of, though."

"Why did you hire him?" I asked.

"We had just lost two stagehands to the army when Old Nick asked if I'd take on his nephew. I knew he'd be worthless based on his uncle's record, and he's completely dim, but it's better to have a useless helper than no help at all."

"Old Nick's nephew? Would it have been Old Nick's idea that Joe sleep in the cellar?" I asked. He looked as though he would fit the clothing we had found.

"I wouldn't be surprised," Gil grumbled.

"He might have sent him down there to guard the exit route for the black-market goods, but that would mean Old Nick was running the black-market operation. Would Joe know where Old Nick's hideouts are?"

"Joe might know where he hides, but he hasn't told any of us. Look, I can't imagine Old Nick having the stamina to run an illegal operation. He's been lazy since the day he was born."

"Then who is running the black market out of the attic here?" I asked.

"As a guess?" Gil asked me.

"Yes."

He considered for a moment. "It just started when this play came to the Regent, so I'd guess one of the actors, the producer, or Mr. Lowe himself. And whoever it is, they or anyone could have told Joe he could live in the cellar since he was bombed out of his home by the Nazis."

"Either to watch the goods or out of kindness," I agreed. "Does Joe have any family beside Old Nick?"

"No one. Or so he told me. I want to get him out and back to work, useless though he is."

"It's too late tonight. We all have to get home before the blackout. I'll go down to Scotland Yard in the morning and talk to the police. By then they should have realized that Joe is not the brains behind anything if he's as dim as you say he is."

* * *

It was almost full dark by the time I reached my father's home. He was in the kitchen finishing dinner and when I walked in asked, "Do you want any dinner? Mrs. Johnson left a vegetable soup and some bread. Has it cooled off any out there?"

I looked in the pot. "I only want half of the soup. Do you want the other half? It's still too hot to eat at the moment."

"Reheat it. It's not edible if it isn't steaming," my father said, proving once again he never listens to me.

I had trouble finding it edible at any temperature, but I soon had it heated again, and cut myself a slice of bread.

My father lowered his paper. "Heard anything from Adam today?"

"Did we get any mail?"

"For some reason, Mrs. Johnson left it on the table in the hallway today."

Rising, I hurried to find I had a letter from Adam and one from Abby. I brought them back to the table and read them as I ate. My father ate hidden behind his newspaper.

I read Adam's letter twice. It was starting to warm up where he was, it would be another few weeks before he'd get leave, and he loved me and missed me terribly.

Abby's letter said she hoped I'd come to visit. The rest was full of the antics of her children, including the two German refugees she and Sir John had adopted, and how they were all busy in the garden and in the fields now that school was out for the summer.

She promised me lots of fresh food off of the ration.

I looked up to see my father had folded his newspaper and had moved his dishes to the sink. "I'll do those when I finish here, shall I?" I said, trying not to sound too annoyed.

"Will Adam be on leave soon?"

"No. So I think I'll take off some time at the beginning of the week and go down to Abby and Sir John's for a day or two."

"Give them my best." My father and his newspaper left the room.

I did the dishes and then sat down in the drawing room in front of an open window to answer both letters. I told Abby I'd catch the first train out on Tuesday morning and I hoped she could arrange to pick me up at the station. *The Stage* would just have to do without me for a day. Then I started writing to Adam.

I complained about the heat and how much I missed him. I wanted to write about the murder of Marshall Lowe, the black- market business being operated out of a theater, and the appearances and disappearances of Old Nick.

But I couldn't. In the end, I told him about the performances I'd seen, then said I'd tell him about the stories I was covering for the newspaper when I saw him next and that I was visiting Abby on Tuesday.

My father walked in and said he thought the weather was quite pleasant and to shut the window when I went upstairs. I told him I would, while thinking how old he'd become if he didn't find the room hot and stuffy.

Once I finished my letter, I again helped myself to my father's stamps and then dragged myself upstairs to bed. Monday I'd start at Scotland Yard, trying to sort out who was being held for murder and who was running the black market out of the Regent Theatre.

Chapter Twenty-One

The next day, Sunday, was miserably boring. The sermon in church was a cure for insomnia, going with my father to his favorite hotel for dinner was delicious if silent, and the rest of the day I sat outside reading or went indoors to take a nap.

Fortunately, the rain waited until the next morning when I left the house, and while I carried an umbrella to keep me dry, there were people out in raincoats as well as using umbrellas. How they stood being bundled up in that heat and humidity, I had no idea.

I went to the main entrance of Scotland Yard and asked to speak to Inspector Dawson or Sergeant Mullins. Mullins appeared after a few minutes and led me toward the basement cells.

"Have you had any luck questioning Joe Landry?"

"He's a dim bulb," Mullins grumbled. "Not much chance of him organizing anything."

"Did he tell you he's Old Nick's nephew?"

"Is he now. Could Old Nick be the brains behind whatever's happening at the Regent?"

"He's sneaky enough. You'd do better if you asked someone who knows him, though." When Mullins turned to look at me, I gave him a smile.

"The inspector's gone down to the cells to start questioning the youngster again. Care to join us?"

"Very much so. Where does Si Chapell stand as far as being released from jail?"

"His solicitor is doing a better job of getting him out than you are." His tone was dry.

"As long as someone is." I smiled again and followed the sergeant through the dark corridors.

When we reached the room where Dawson was questioning Joe Landry, the first thing I noticed was how puzzled Joe looked. Mullins only needed to give Dawson a single nod to get him to allow me to question his prisoner.

I sat across from the young man and said, "Do you remember me, Joe? I'm with *The Stage* newspaper and I'm a friend of Marnie's."

He nodded.

Being in a basement room on a gloomy day, Dawson had already turned on the overhead light and as it was cool, it was quite pleasant despite the hard, wooden furniture. "We've been looking for Old Nick. He's quite a trickster, isn't he? Never around when we're looking for him. He's your uncle, isn't he?"

Another nod.

"We've looked everywhere we could think of, and we can't find him if he's not backstage. Do you know where he hides out, Joe?"

He hesitated before nodding this time.

"Where is he? I need to talk to him."

"In the East End around the corner from where I used to live. The whole area's full of bomb sites. He's in a damaged house on McDill Street."

"And he goes in and out through the cellars under the stage?"

An enthusiastic nod this time.

"How do I keep missing him? I look for him every time I'm at the Regent, but I miss him half the time. The cast and backstage crew never see him when they're looking for him either. Have you seen him recently?"

Joe nodded again. "He brought me an apple yesterday before the performance. I'm not the only one who's seen him."

"Who else has seen him, Joe?" I kept my voice calm. If I frightened him, I was afraid he'd stop talking.

"Mike Harris and Miss Carroll. And Miss Marnie."

I glanced over to see Dawson's eyebrows rise. He was probably wondering the same thing I was. What game was Marnie playing with us?

"Meanwhile, you've been living in the cellar. Don't you find it cold down there?"

He looked down in silence, shrugging.

The inspector was about to speak, but I gestured him to stay quiet. "It's all right that you were sleeping in the cellar. The Nazis bombed you out of your home. Where else were you going to go? And you work there. We understand."

He looked up at me then.

"But it must be very cold sleeping down in the cellar."

"It's all right. I found a blanket."

"Where did you find the blanket, Joe?" I hoped it led to a clue about the people running the black market in fabric up in the attic.

"In a house that was bombed."

That didn't get us anywhere. Dawson glanced at me, telling me to hurry up. "Did you think of sleeping down there all on your own or did your uncle Nick suggest it?"

"He did."

"And you weren't too cold? Or wet?" I thought it was damp down there.

He shook his head.

"It isn't that cold," Inspector Dawson said.

"What did Old Nick tell you to do when you were on your own in the theater after it was closed up for the night?" I asked.

"He said I could guard the scenery and stuff," Joe said quietly.

"And did you?" I asked.

He nodded, looking pleased.

"Who went up into the attic where the old stuff is?" I asked.

He looked down and shook his head.

"Who was in the theater late at night after everyone else left?"

He shook his head as if he was a mule.

"Weren't you lonely in the theater late at night?"

Another headshake.

I looked at Dawson and held my hands palm up. I was out of ideas and out of my depth.

"Thank you, Mrs. Redmond," Dawson said and motioned with his head for me to leave.

"Mr. Chapell?" I asked him as I rose.

"Has a hearing at three this afternoon. His solicitor arranged it. I suspect he'll be released. This would have been easier if he'd been honest with us about where he was and when." Dawson's sour expression had returned.

"Thank you." I left and went to *The Stage* office. Mr. Bridges was working on the next issue's layout when I arrived. "Si may be released after a court hearing this afternoon. With any luck, we'll see him here tomorrow morning. In the meantime, I'm going over to the Regent and try to make sense out of some of these puzzles."

"What do we want to cover this week, if Si doesn't get out?"

"There's a Proms performance at Albert Hall on Saturday led by Sir Henry Wood. Would you prefer to cover that story or Chekhov's *Uncle Vanya* on the BBC?"

"The Proms," Mr. Bridges said with enthusiasm.

"Great. It's yours. Telephone them and tell them you're covering their performance for the newspaper and either the box office or the ushers will show you to your seat. Now I'm off to the Regent."

"And their crimes," he replied with a grin. "Good luck solving them."

I needed all the luck I could get. I walked to the Regent in another downpour and now the wind had picked up. People were bundled up, but all I needed was my umbrella. I hurried, so at least I didn't get soaked, but neither was I roasting.

Marnie and Nora were entering the stage door just as I arrived. Marnie clasped my hand once we were inside and shed of rain gear as she said, "My solicitor has a hearing for Si this afternoon. He has every hope of getting him released."

"You care a great deal for him."

"Of course. I've known him forever."

"I've known lots of people forever, but I don't think I'd be paying for legal help to get them out of jail, murder charge or no murder charge."

She stared at me. "How many of them would you leave your husband for?"

"So, the rumors are true."

"That depends on which version of the rumors you have heard." Marnie strolled toward her dressing room.

I caught a glimpse of the door to the attic opening, so I hurried down the hall. But when I reached the door, no one was in the hallway and no one passed me, so they must have gone upstairs. I tried the door handle. The door swung open, throwing light onto the stairs.

Two voices floated down to me from the top of the stairs for a moment before they fell silent. Then a woman's voice said "Here" and footsteps clattered down the stairs.

"Can't you mind your own business?" Jane Barber asked.

I noticed her arms were empty, but one hand carried the big torch that sat by the door in the attic.

"No," I told her with a smile. "That's why I'm a reporter."

"Try it. You might find you enjoy it." Jane reached past me, pulled the door shut, and locked it.

I decided to position myself where I could see her reemerge with whoever she went upstairs with. I suspected they were our black-market storekeepers, and with the matinee performance in an hour or so, whoever had gone up there would have to come back down and soon.

While I stood there waiting, Gil Baker came up to me. "Are they releasing Joe?"

"I don't know. He told them where to find Old Nick, and I think the police are more interested in Old Nick than in a suggestible young man such as Joe."

"You know, I thought I saw Old Nick, just a glimpse of him, earlier today when I first arrived."

"When was that?"

"I don't know. Eleven. Eleven-thirty."

"Where did you see him?"

"Backstage." He pointed. "Near the cellar door."

"Is he still on the payroll here?"

"Why wouldn't he be? They've not replaced him, except for the bobbies always hanging around. Don't forget, Art Jackson likes him."

"Between the murder and some—other matters, there's a reason those bobbies are hanging around," I told him.

"I guess we'll just have to do the matinee one short for

the scene switches and then we'll see," Gil told me and walked off, calling the other two stagehands.

Digging through my bag, I found my notebook and began scribbling notes while standing half hidden by scenery. Jane Barber walked past me, followed a half minute later by Michael Harris, but I didn't acknowledge either of them as I concentrated on my notebook. I wasn't certain they noticed me.

Inspector Dawson noticed the intent gaze I followed them with, though. He waited until they walked past him and then came over to me. "Harris and Jane Barber were both upstairs?"

"Yes. With their own key."

"We know who to watch now." He gave me a nod and walked off.

I went back to Marnie's dressing room. "Why didn't you leave your husband for Si?"

She held completely still for a moment while Nora did her eye makeup for the afternoon's performance. Then she swiveled around to look at me, one eye plain and one heavily made up for the stage. "What makes you think I didn't?"

"You never married him, even after you were free of Marshall Lowe, however you did that. I'm certain divorce laws used to be much more difficult than they are now."

"I didn't divorce Marshall. He divorced me. Much easier all the way around. Some friends kept it from reaching the newspapers, and we all resumed our lives, sooner or later."

Suddenly, some things became clearer. "Was Sir Henry

one of those friends?"

"He wasn't Sir Henry then, but yes, he was. He's always been a good friend to Si, and through him, to me. Newcastle boys stick together, you see."

"Still, you apparently didn't stay with Si for long."

"If we'd stayed together longer, we'd never have remained friends." She turned back then for Nora to work on her stage makeup on the other eye.

"What are you not telling me?" I asked.

"I've answered every one of your questions fully and truthfully." Marnie put some drama into her tone.

"It's what I haven't guessed that is at the heart of this. Am I right?" I watched her face in the mirror. She looked back at me with a complete lack of expression. Except her eyes. They showed her anger.

"Do let me know how Si's hearing turns out. I'm hoping they release him." Then she went back to having Nora paint her face.

"So do I. And then I hope one of you tells me what this big secret is." I hurried out of the dressing room and nearly collided with the inspector.

"You don't know what Chapell is hiding. I thought you knew," he said.

"Do you know?"

"I thought it was the sinful nature of their relationship before the Great War. I've been as wrong as you."

"What would they..." I stopped myself from continuing my sentence aloud. *Be hiding thirty years later.* There was only one thing. A child. A child who could still be hurt by the revelation that they were illegitimate.

Who could be injured by such a discovery at this age? At my age. A vicar? A politician? A child adopted by an aristocratic family who didn't know their background? Someone who couldn't bear up under the scrutiny of the press and public?

If Scotland Yard found out about this child, it would become public knowledge, as most things did that reached the police department. I certainly wasn't going to suggest this to them and send them out looking for the child.

But more important, what did it have to do with Marshall Lowe's murder?

"What? I can see you've thought of something," Inspector Dawson said.

"No. Besides, you'll have your hands full stopping Jane and Harris and their black-market scheme." When he didn't reply, I said, "I know you saw them come out of the attic. No one would go up into that inferno without a good reason."

"That's a matter of watching and then closing the net. In the meantime, Old Nick is missing. He's moved out of what's left of the house in the East End. He has a record of being involved with smuggling from the Continent before the war. He's been suspected of being involved in the black market for some time."

"The head stagehand saw him before noon today," I told him.

"Here?" He sounded as if it was a demand.

I nodded.

"Then they must be getting ready to move their goods. We've left them their parcels undisturbed to carry out a transfer, taking enough photographs for evidence for a search warrant. Then we can catch everyone red-handed. Nothing will bring Old Nick out into the open as much as a big sale of goods he's stolen," the inspector said.

"May I watch your men take them down?" That would make a good article for the *Daily Premier*.

"No."

Chapter Twenty-Two

Dawson and Mullins walked off, no doubt to set up their capture of the thieves now that they'd discovered the black-market goods and another escape route out of the theater. They were welcome to all their plotting. I wanted to talk to Old Nick. He'd hinted right from the start that he knew all of his contemporaries' secrets.

I wanted to know what he knew about Si and Marnie, and whether it would lead them to kill.

The only question was, how to catch him before the police did. I was pretty certain he was using the stairs down to the cellars to come in and out of the theater. Maybe the best place to wait for him would be in the cellars during a performance.

After I made sure he was nowhere near his proper location of employment at the stage door, I went back to Marnie's dressing room. She and Nora glanced my way and then went back to getting Marnie ready for the matinee performance.

"I'm going down into the cellar to try to meet up with Old Nick. Apparently, that is how he comes and goes without anyone seeing him. If the police or Si want to see me, that's where I'll be."

"And if no one sees you in the next few days, we'll be sure to tell the police," Nora said, giving me a dirty look.

"Thank you." If Si was released at his three o'clock hearing, I felt certain the first place he'd come would be here to see Marnie. She'd paid for the solicitor, after all. He'd probably arrive between performances and that was when I wanted to hear what was said between them.

After making doubly certain that no one had seen Old Nick by his spot at the stage door and he wasn't hiding in the storeroom, I took the stairs down into the cool cellars. They were damp and dark, except for a little light generated by a few weak lightbulbs and shafts of light at a distance from bomb holes gaping open to the sky.

It wasn't particularly scary, at least not in the daytime. This was the first time in weeks I'd had any lengthy respite from being boiling hot, so I was enjoying my time down there. If only it didn't smell of damp rot with a faint whiff of sewers. Now all I needed was for Old Nick to appear.

I settled down to wait on the wooden stairs. I had tossed and turned in the heat the night before, so my eyelids were heavy in the peaceful, dark cellar. I could hear the applause at the end of each scene from up above me, but no one approached the stairs.

Maybe this wasn't such a bright way to find Old Nick sneaking in or out of the theater.

It was nearly five when I gave up and slowly climbed the steps to the stage level of the theater. If Si had been released, he should have been there with Marnie. I quietly walked to the doorway into her dressing room and then leaned on the wall.

I could hear voices inside, but they were muffled. I slid a little closer, hoping I'd hear something intelligible. Instead, the door swung open and Old Nick came out.

"Oi. What are you doing here?"

I was so surprised at seeing him it took me a moment to make my mouth work. "Looking for you and wondering if Si was released from jail."

"See for yourself." Old Nick walked away as I stuck my head in the dressing room to find Si holding Marnie's hand as if he were proposing to her.

"Livvy," Si exclaimed, turning to me. "I've been released. They aren't admitting I'm no longer a suspect, but I'm free for the time being. Now, what are you doing here?"

"I'm trying to find out what the big secret is between you, Marnie, and Marshall Lowe, and whether it was worth killing to keep quiet."

"It isn't. Neither of us killed him."

"I'm not going to tell your secret, Si, but if I'm going to help clear your name, you have to be honest with me."

"Oh, look. Now I've ruined my makeup," Marnie said, tears running down her face. "Nora, you'll have to help me redo for the evening performance."

"It's all right. Marnie, it's not your fault," Si said.

"Yes, it is. It must be." She sobbed harder.

He put his arms around her. "No, my darling girl. No."

The sorrow passing between the two of them filled the room.

Nora set down her sewing and said, "We'll mend your face for the evening performance. And you," she said, rounding on me, "need to leave."

"I need to know everything if I'm going to stop Dawson from bringing more charges against Si. He's been released, not exonerated."

"He wouldn't kill anybody," Nora said, moving closer.

"Prove it." I stared back at her with as much anger as she aimed at me.

Marnie's stage-modulated tones grabbed our attention. "Ladies, please. Nora, Si, I know you're trying to spare my feelings, but Livvy does have a point. There is no sense in you being in jail, my love, if she can prove you innocent. Come back here after tonight's performance, and I'll tell you all."

Nora snorted, her arms crossed over her chest.

"She thinks she needs to know. Maybe she does. After tonight's performance. Now, go, and let me get ready." Marnie began to mop her face with a handkerchief.

Si squeezed her shoulder as he rose and then led me out of the dressing room. "She's being very brave," he said.

"No doubt she is, but you've been braver, keeping her secret the whole way to jail and back."

"It's my secret too."

Before I could respond, I heard Gil Baker call out, "Thank goodness. You were missed this afternoon."

I looked over to see the young stagehand, Joe Landry, walk down the hall from the stage door. "Where's Old Nick?"

he asked.

"He was around a few minutes ago," Si told him.

"Don't worry about Old Nick. Worry about which ropes to pull to move scenery tonight," Baker told his assistant.

"That means the police aren't holding anyone for Marshall Lowe's death now," I told Si. "I don't think they'll ever solve his murder."

"Which will leave Marnie and me, and a lot of other people, in a sort of limbo. You have to solve this, Livvy, especially after you hear our secret."

"I'll certainly try," I promised.

"Come on, let's go back to the office and then get our tea." We went to *The Stage* office in Bush House, where Mr. Bridges was finishing up for the day. The two men got along immediately with their shared love of variety theater and their knowledge of newspapers over the past thirty years. Si invited him to tea also, and Mr. Bridges was immediately ready to go.

While they had a full meal, I only had a little soup and some tea, and even then my stomach was trying to rebel. I decided it must be from the time spent in the damp, smelly cellar under the theater.

Afterward, Mr. Bridges went to a performance of the Proms and we went back to the Regent Theatre. Now that I had a promise that I would be told this secret that might or might not be worth killing for, I wasn't letting Si out of my sight.

Old Nick was minding the stage door and smelling of

spirits. Both Si and I said hello; Old Nick grunted. The bobby standing nearby raised his eyebrows at Si before acknowledging my greeting.

I followed Si to Marnie's dressing room, where she was now ready to go onstage. We both wished her luck in the form of a broken leg, Nora looked daggers at me, and we headed for the side of the stage where we could watch the performance.

I had forgotten Si hadn't seen this play through from start to finish. I enjoyed his enjoyment in what had become a better play since Bud Cosby had taken over the direction. It wasn't sophisticated and Bud was no Shakespeare, but for a domestic comedy, it was quite good.

Marnie went through her "I'm unappreciated" speech, sending the audience into gales of laughter, and then she pulled her first disappearing act. As she came offstage on our side, Si pulled her in for a hug and a peck on the cheek and whispered, "Brilliant."

She gestured us to follow her away from the stage. "It's much improved as a play since Bud took over Marshall's job. Straight forward hide-and-seek with a wittier dialogue."

"I guess it's even further away from the play that Philip Bernard originally wrote?" I asked.

"Oh, yes. I doubt if he were here tonight he'd recognize this as his tragedy," Marnie said. "Poor man. I guess he just couldn't get past his early life in the East End, but after he'd written his play, he had to keep reliving his misery every time he tried to sell the play or see our rehearsals with the way

Marshall butchered it."

"Did he?"

"Oh, yes." Marnie made a dramatic sweeping move with one hand. "If you had read it originally, a year ago, at the beginning rehearsals while Marshall worked out what he really wanted, you'd understand. He used Bernard's characters, who were people he'd grown up with, and changed their nature completely. Joking and laughing, making them characters in a comedy. The poor boy couldn't stand it."

"But before he died, Lowe kept insisting he was saving Bernard's play for after the war and this comedy had nothing to do with his play. I heard him," I said.

"Lowe always could lie to your face and make it sound as if it was the truth," Si said.

"At least he changed the characters. Three daughters and their husbands and boyfriends. A vicar. No sons."

"But my character, the mother-in-law, stayed widowed. Fortunately, not by her own hand in our version," Marnie said. "And Marshall kept saying, at least recently, 'You sold the play, so stop complaining.'"

"What a sensitive human being," I muttered. I'd already learned how unpleasant he could be. He seemed to seek out his murder.

"Back in a minute," Marnie said to Si and hurried over to the wings. We tiptoed up behind her. A minute later, she went on for one of her brief appearances, confusing her family with a note this time.

She came back offstage in time for two of her daughters to be puzzled in the most laugh-provoking manner. Si was laughing as hard as the audience.

And then it hit me. "You're the heroine of this play, Marnie," I whispered.

"Of course. I'm always the lead."

"No. Philip Bernard must have written the original play with your character as the villain. Marshall made you the heroine. No wonder Bernard was distraught."

She thought for a moment. "You're right. Nothing any of us can do now, but you're right."

"When exactly did Bernard kill himself?" Si asked, frowning.

"Right before Lowe was murdered. The night before, or very early that morning," Marnie told him.

"Shortly after you returned to London?" I asked.

She nodded, her mind already on the next scene as she moved to the edge of the wings. Si followed her eagerly. I followed more slowly, an idea trying to grow in my mind.

He'd only received the money for the play a couple of days before his death. What did that mean?

And then Marnie was onstage, working her magic on Si and the audience as she verbally fenced with the vicar and drawing me in as the idea floated away.

The scene was a great success. Marnie slipped away again just before Diana, as her daughter, and Bud Cosby, as her son-in-law, came on and danced to the swing music that had caused Wanda Thomas to break her leg in rehearsal.

Because of sabotage. Sabotage before Bernard was paid for his play.

Marnie headed for her dressing room since she had a few minutes to sit down. Nora had a cup of tea ready for her as soon as she entered. She sat back, savoring the tea with her eyes closed.

"No one ever considers how hard it is on the actors when they have two performances a day," Nora muttered at me while Si sat with his hand resting on Marnie's arm.

The peace only lasted for a few minutes before Nora warned Marnie it was time to get back to work. She set down her teacup and headed back down the hall with Si at her side.

Ahead, I could see Baker and his assistants readying to reset the stage for another scene in the garden. This meant raising the heavy interior backdrop and tying it off as well as moving some small plants and a bench onto the stage and removing the drawing room sofa. The stagehands were figures hurrying soundlessly around in the dark while actors hovered on the edge of the stage, ready to go on.

I was close enough to feel the whoosh of air a moment before the scenery crashed down, followed by a howl of pain.

"Close the curtain," a man's voice shouted. "Close the curtain!"

Chapter Twenty-Three

When the curtain was closed and the backstage lights were turned up, I first saw Bert Lanshire, the props man, on the floor, one foot caught under the heavy wooden scenery flat for the interior scenes of the play that should have been up in the rafters. Bud Cosby was on the floor, his jacket caught under the deadly scenery, the rest of him next to it, with Robbie Day on top of him. Close to them was Joe Landry, crushed under the weight of the backdrop.

I'd seen dead bodies before and had various reactions. This time, I nearly knocked Old Nick out of the way as I began to dash toward the stage door in my haste to get sick in the alley.

When I reentered the backstage, I found Vic Graybell pressed against the outer wall of the building storeroom, shaking uncontrollably and howling. Old Nick was holding him up. I went over to them, and with Vic between us, managed to move him to Old Nick's ratty chair. I pushed Vic's head between his knees and told him to breathe deeply.

Once he began to take deep breaths, he stopped howling and his shaking slowed.

I walked as far as where Bud Cosby and Robbie Day were

now sitting up on the backstage floor. "Thank you," Bud murmured in a voice unlike his own assured, stage voice and shook Robbie's hand. Both of them were sweating, but not as much as Burt Lanshire, who was prone on the floor now and unconscious or dead from the shock. At least his foot appeared attached.

The bobby met the reinforcements at the door. Now that the police had arrived, they made certain we all knew they were in charge. Gil Baker was arguing with Inspector Dawson about the condition of a rope and whether it had been in its present state for a long time or only that evening.

I walked past them to Marnie's dressing room. Si rose when I entered and said, "Are you all right? You're gone all pale."

The room was very bright and out of focus. "Just sick. I need to settle down before I go back to listening to the police. And I need to call in the story to the *Daily Premier*."

"You're not going anywhere, young lady. Sit down and put your head between your knees," Nora said, leading me to a chair and pushing me into it.

After a few minutes I felt surprisingly better. When I looked around, I realized Si was no longer there. "Where's...?"

"Doing your job. Now, pull yourself together," Nora said.

Si came in a moment later with Gil Baker. "Gil says the rope was sawn almost through at the sandbag end."

"It was fine at the end of the matinee. That's when I check ropes and sandbags and such," Gil told me. "Because they get all their wear and tear during a show now that we're done with rehearsals. Everything was fine with that rope, with all the ropes. I know. I checked."

"Did Inspector Dawson not believe you?"

Baker began to pace across the small dressing room. "No. I don't know if he thinks I sawed through that rope myself or just didn't look, but he doesn't believe anything I say."

"He's looking for an easy answer to both murders, but I think it's going to be complicated. Even though Joe was the victim and I think he was aiding the black-market ring with their goods in the attic, while Marshall Lowe's death had nothing to do with the black market, I think the two deaths are still somehow related. Just not in a way we've worked out so far." I felt better, but no further along in solving our mysteries.

I watched Gil Baker propel his large body back and forth across the small space. "Tell me everything you know about Joe Landry," I said.

He paused his pacing to think. "He's lived all his life in the East End. His father left, died, whatever, when he was small, so his mother raised him. Old Nick was a relative, an uncle or cousin, and helped them out."

When he stopped, I asked, "Anything else?"

"He wasn't bright, but he was willing to work. He was a good lad. He didn't deserve this."

"No one does," Si said. I wondered if he thought of Marshall Lowe when he said those words.

"Could Bert Lanshire have been the target?"

"I wouldn't think so," Baker said. "There's a lot of movement on the stage at that time, between props and the set. The scenery could have come down on anybody. It happened when the rope broke."

"Who worked that rope?"

"Joe did."

"So, he could be expected to be near anything that fell when the rope broke?"

"Yes, as long as it broke while we were changing scenes."

"Why didn't the lad notice the rope had been cut?" Si asked before I could.

Baker quit pacing. "He might have, but if his job was to pull on that rope, that's what he would do. The state of the rope wouldn't concern him unless you gave him very definite instructions to check the rope. Since I did the checking after every performance, I didn't see any reason to tell him to. Only when you gave him explicit directions could you count on him doing his tasks. He was a good lad. Just a bit slow."

"Who knew what his tasks were?" I asked.

"Everyone associated with the play." Baker looked at the actors. "Well, anyone paying any attention."

"It was done the same every time?"

"Until Bud Cosby changed scenes around, and then we had to change our tasks to match. But he hadn't done that lately."

"What's lately?" Si asked.

"It's been a few days. Since before the police took Joe

away for questioning."

"Thanks, Mr. Baker. I know you have a lot to do tonight and tomorrow since you're down a man..." I began.

"Two."

"What?" I was confused.

"Bert won't be fit to do his job for weeks. I'll have to replace him in the meantime. If they don't close this theater down." Baker shook his head. "Two murders and a black-market ring? The authorities must be having a fit."

"Plays must pass the censor, and theaters can only be open by license," Si explained to me. "There's a great deal of government censorship under the Theaters Act of 1843. Films and revues don't have to jump through all these hoops. Plays and theaters hosting plays do. Something as awful as this should have them pulling our permit."

Marnie, who'd been silent all this time, said, "We have to find the killer. Otherwise, we're all out of a job and I can't afford it. Well, none of us can."

"How do you propose to solve two murders?" Si asked. He looked at Marnie as if he knew she'd have the answer.

"We need a new props person. What about Livvy? It would give her reason to be around for every performance, listen to everyone's conversation, and watch people."

"I already have a job," I said with some annoyance.

"Now that I have Mr. Bridges, he and I can run the newspaper and you can work as props man for now. Gil can show you how to do the job and what's needed, and then you just have to lay everything out in the right place and stay away from falling scenery." Si looked as if he'd solved everything.

"I can't be here for tomorrow's performance. I have to be out of town," was only my first objection.

"Fine, you can start Wednesday afternoon. We only have an evening performance that day. One afternoon is enough to teach you every task and object that the props man handles," Baker said as if that settled it. "I can cover both jobs for one night."

"If the police let you have a performance tomorrow night. What if—?" I was about to ask what would happen if the police shut down the theater until another play with other performers and stagehands could be found. That would be the end of our sleuthing and any chance of finding the killer.

At that moment, I noticed Inspector Dawson and Sergeant Mullins in the doorway, looking grim.

"The theater will be dark tomorrow night, but you can proceed on Wednesday if Mrs. Redmond is your props man. Since she has been assigned by someone higher up in the government to assist us in this investigation, this assures us she'll be right here assisting us." Dawson's expression was smug. I knew he didn't care for having me assigned to help prove Si's innocence, but this told me how much he really didn't enjoy my company.

"Well, if Mr. Chapell is no longer considered a suspect in Marshall Lowe's death, then—?"

"He's been released. He hasn't been cleared," the

inspector said. "We're closing off the theater until Wednesday afternoon. Right now, everyone needs to leave before the blackout."

The police then did an efficient job of emptying the backstage area and posting guards. The inspector held me back until last so that he could tell me, "We'll expect a report from you daily and a warning if anything untoward happens."

"You will be keeping a presence backstage besides me, I hope. I have no training and no arrest powers," I reminded him.

"Don't worry. We won't leave you here on your own."

* * *

All of this I relayed to Abby the next day when she picked me up at the train station. I decided I'd better tell her quickly before her four sons, two natural and two orphans adopted from the Kindertransport I'd been on, demanded my attention.

Heinrich, now known as Henry, the youngest of the four, came running out from the barns as we pulled up by the house. "Lady Abby, Lady Abby, they want Matthew to work part time on some engineering marvel while he does the rest of his university work. And hello, Cousin Livvy!"

He nearly crushed me with his hug. I hadn't seen him since what we now hoped was the last weekend of the Blitz, when my flat had been blown up by a German bomb while I'd visited Summersby House more than two months before. I thought he'd already grown another inch.

Abby told Henry to carry my case upstairs while she and

I went into the drawing room. He did as asked with the enthusiasm of a sports crowd and the grace of a hippopotamus. Abby winced as something went bang and then shrugged. "Nothing the other three didn't crash into at one time or another."

Matthew, the oldest and the only one at university, came in from the direction of the kitchen with a half-eaten apple in one hand and what appeared to be a letter in the other. "Mum, look! I have a place in a research facility in Cambridge this coming year while I do my classes. I can stay enrolled in my engineering course!"

Mother and son hugged and then I congratulated him before he ran out waving his letter.

"And the other two?" I asked.

"Mark will be in his next to last year in boarding school. We're going to send Gerhard there in the autumn. We think he and Henry can be separated now, and his English is excellent."

"You and Sir John have worked wonders with both those boys."

"It's been our pleasure. They're an integral part of the family now. We can't imagine life without them." Abby smiled. "And they are all happy to see you this weekend. The first since you were bombed out of your home. How have you been, living with your father again after all these years?"

I groaned. "About as well as you'd expect. At least Adam has been home twice in the past two months or more and my father adores Adam."

"Peace has reigned twice?"

"Conversation has broken out twice. Otherwise, the house is eerily silent, even when we're in the same room."

"Any chance you can rent a flat near Adam's camp?"

"Apparently not. It's in the middle of nowhere, plus the married instructors are all trying to bring their families to a town twenty miles away without luck. And we don't have any children."

Henry came in from the kitchen munching on an apple. "I'm glad you were here the weekend all the bombs blew up. Otherwise, you could have been under the rubble instead of down here safe in your bed."

"I'm glad, too," I told him. "How will it be this autumn with only you at home while Gerhard's away at school?"

"I'm not a baby anymore. And Ger passed his exams, so he should go away to school with Mark."

"Is that what you're calling him now? Ger?"

Henry nodded and headed back toward the kitchen.

Abby laughed and said, "I'm afraid so."

Henry popped back out. "Dinner is ready. I'll tell the others."

Within a few minutes, the boys had all scrubbed, I had greeted Sir John, and we all sat down around the dining table. Abby's longtime maid, Gladys, served us the soup course and then went back to the kitchen. One taste of the vegetable soup and I knew Abby's longtime cook had also stayed despite the call of better earnings in the factories.

Somehow, the vaguely rancid smell of the soup didn't

match the good taste.

I was able to eat most of it, although more slowly than the boys, who all powered through their soup as if they hadn't eaten in a month. Then they all started to talk to me at once until Sir John called them to order.

Through some signal I didn't see, Gerhard went first. "I'm going away to school in September with Mark. And everyone's calling me 'Ger' now."

Matthew said, "You've heard my good news already."

Mark told me how well he was doing in his foreign language courses and that he hoped to help the war effort with his talent.

Henry said, "I'm raising rabbits, and we eat them! We're having one for dinner today."

I completely lost my appetite.

When Henry's creature came out from the kitchen a moment later in a casserole, the smell made me ill. I ran to the toilet.

Chapter Twenty-Four

I heard chairs scrape behind me, as all well-brought-up men stood when a lady left the room, but I didn't have time to say "Excuse me, please." I managed to make it in time and after I washed my face and hands, returned to the table.

"I apologize," I said into their startled faces as I sat.

"Henry's proclamations frequently make me ill, too," Matthew joked.

"I'm sorry," Henry said, nearly in tears. I had no idea what his elder brothers had said to him while I was gone.

"It's not your fault, Henry," Abby said. "I think Cousin Livvy is keeping a secret."

I looked at her in dawning recognition. "Am I?"

"When was Adam last home?"

"Only two weeks ago."

"No, that wouldn't be it. The time before?"

"Near the end of May."

"That's probably it."

"That's probably what?" Henry asked.

Sir John, who had been studying the ceiling since his wife started quizzing me, said, "Later," in a voice that brooked no argument.

Mark and Gerhard glanced at each other, looked at me, and began to giggle. Matthew, closest to Mark, punched him in the ribs. Poor Henry looked completely confused.

I felt the same way. I thought you just knew when you were carrying a child. Apparently not. I tried in vain to remember when I'd last had my monthly courses. Abby and I were going to have a long, private conversation after dinner. I took a sip of water and said, "Abby, have the boys been helping you in the kitchen garden?"

"Very willingly." She smiled at each of the boys in turn and then she asked me if I remembered a friend of hers who lived on a neighboring farm. When I said I did, she went into a long story about the neighbor moving into the village and leaving the farm to her younger son and his family.

By this time, everyone else had finished their casserole. Gladys cleared the table and brought in our pudding. It was soft, odorless, and tasted of berries. I was able to eat mine without difficulty.

I saw Henry watching me eat dessert without eating dinner and then look from Abby to Sir John with a puzzled look. This was something I was sure he wasn't allowed to do. I didn't plan to explain anything to him. That was Sir John's job.

Matthew also saw his expression and as soon as Henry finished his pudding, said, "May we be excused to go out and play ball?"

Sir John said, "Of course," almost before Matthew stopped speaking.

The older three boys stood and walked outside, breaking into a run when they reached the back door. Henry hesitated for a moment, looked around as if he wanted to say something, and took off after them.

As soon as we heard the back door shut, Sir John said, "I'll leave you to it," and fled the room.

"Shall we have our coffee in the small drawing room?" Abby made arrangements for it to be brought to us and we went to the most feminine of the downstairs rooms.

We took overstuffed chairs across the cold fireplace from each other and settled in to wait for the coffee. Once it was delivered, Abby played mother and then we had a sip of our ersatz coffee.

Abby made a face and then said, "Tell me. Are you with child?"

"I have no idea. I've never been before. Will I be sick for the entire time? I need to keep working, at least as long as I am able."

Abby then explained all the variations of reactions I might experience. By the time she finished, I was completely confused.

"You need to see your doctor," Abby continued. "Not only do you need to be checked out to see if everything is all right, he's the one to sign the papers to get you more rations, both now and after the baby arrives."

"How long can I keep working?"

"Don't you mean, how long can you hide this from your father?"

I nodded. I realized I was afraid to tell him. "He'll be thrilled for Adam and be certain from the start that it's a boy, but any noise the child makes will be my fault. How long can I keep working?"

"Until the child is obvious."

"After that, I may be hiding out here to avoid my father and his annoyance. Until the child is ready to arrive."

"And afterward? It will still be winter. This may not be the place you want to be."

I looked at her and shrugged. "I don't know." That was the truth. I was still in shock.

Abby smiled at me. "Talk to your friend Esther. She has two small children. Ask her how she handles screaming infants and how this experience you'll be going through feels."

"Esther has a cook and a nanny." My shoulders slumped even more.

"Not that I'd know where you'd find one, but do you think Sir Ronald would hire a nanny?"

"Never. And I don't have the money. Even then, we'd never keep an infant quiet enough to suit my father." The more real this baby felt, the more frightened I became.

"Are you happy about the baby?" Abby asked.

"I thought I'd be. Now I'm just afraid."

"Write to Adam. Talk to your father. And give yourself time to adjust. Everything will be all right."

I nodded, hoping she was right.

"Now, what would you want to do?"

"Sit on the terrace and watch the boys play ball." I smiled at her, and she returned a look of sharing a secret.

She gave me a hug and we went out to see the older boys helping Henry with his stance batting in cricket. We had a lovely afternoon cheering them on, joined by Sir John.

"Does Adam know?" he murmured during one raucous moment.

His wife shot him a look and shook her head.

We went inside when it was time for a cold supper, stopping first for everyone to clean up before they came to the table. I had a little cold roast chicken on some bread with a green salad. None of the food carried a smell that made me ill, and the boys all acted as if they'd forgotten the earlier incident.

After we'd eaten, they went into the study to listen to the wireless while we three adults went to the drawing room for more ersatz coffee. I asked if I could have tea instead.

"Of course, but you'll have to forgive if it's weak and bland."

"Oh, Abby, you have to realize that everything you serve is better than what we can get in town."

We discussed rationing and how the war with Russia was going for the Germans. I told them about the plays I had seen working for *The Stage* and how the next day I would learn to be a props man in a play, leaving out that I was meant to be on site to try to catch a murderer. What the famous Marnie Keller was really like and how the police didn't enjoy needing to cooperate with me to keep Sir Malcolm happy.

When we went upstairs, I nearly fell asleep before I was ready for bed, and then I slept as if I didn't have a care in the world.

I woke up the next morning wondering how I'd tell my father.

Sir John, Abby, and the boys were busy with the farm, and directly after breakfast, Abby drove me to the station before running an errand. She wished me luck, we hugged, and then I went onto the platform to wait for the train.

* * *

After arrival at the train station and vegetable soup at an ABC lunch counter, I walked over to the Regent for my training as a props man. Gil Baker was patient with me, although he thought my lack of attention was due to my trying to catch a murderer, not worrying about a possible pregnancy. I wasn't about to correct him.

Bud Cosby, as the director as well as an actor in the play, checked over the props table. He appeared surprised when he learned I would be filling in for Bert Lanshire, but assured me it wouldn't be for too long since Lanshire was making a speedy recovery. The scenery had come down flat on his foot, breaking small bones but not damaging nerves or blood vessels.

The stagehands and a few of the actors had arrived before Inspector Dawson and Sergeant Mullins walked into the backstage area. "Good," the inspector said. "Call me if anything suspicious happens. We'll be around for the performance."

"Is Old Nick on the stage door or one of your men?" I asked.

"Both tonight." Then the inspector stepped closer. "Keep your eyes open," he said to me in a low voice. "We've heard the black-market goods will be moved tonight."

"Are they still in the attic?" I murmured back.

"We checked late this morning. They were then."

"Do you have anyone posted in the cellar? With all those underground passages from old buildings and closed Tube lines, that would allow them to come up to street level at a distance in various places."

Dawson looked grim. "At both ends."

He walked off as Marnie, Nora, and Si came over to the props table. "It looks as if everything is ready," Marnie said. "You may have found a new calling."

"I don't think so. Mr. Baker is about to fire me before my first performance," I told her.

"No," he said, "she's doing fine. And if anything gets confused, we're all here to help her."

"Just don't leave the table once it's ready for a performance," Si said. Everyone nodded in agreement.

"That's the quickest way to get something mixed up or missing," Baker added.

"Marnie," I said as she began to walk off, "you promised to tell me something I need to know just before Joe Landry was killed. When were you going to tell me?"

"I'll try to tell you tonight if nothing else goes wrong. Don't worry. I'll keep my word," she said with a smile that had entranced audiences for decades.

The others went to get ready or to do their tasks, leaving me alone. I'd taken notes on the various props and they sat on the table in neat order, all the bits and pieces that would be carried out on stage.

I looked around, watching the activity build as it grew closer in time for the curtain to rise. And then the magic moment arrived and everyone began to move through their well- rehearsed words and steps.

When we reached intermission, Gil Baker smiled and gave me a nod of approval. I readied the props table for the second act as he'd shown me while stagehands changed scenery and lighting and actors changed costumes.

I glanced over and noticed two large men who appeared to be stagehands come up from the cellar and walk down the hall. I looked around but didn't see any of the bobbies or Inspector Dawson. I hoped they were in position, out of sight, as Jane Barber and Vic Graybell crowded around the table, taking the props they needed for the kitchen scene at the beginning of act two, and blocking my view. The actors stayed there, hovering over me, until the curtain rose and then they went on stage.

Only then could I look around again for a policeman or the two men I hadn't been able to identify. No one was in sight.

I had no choice. I had to leave the table. I crossed behind the stage to the door where there was a bobby, but Old Nick had taken off again.

"Where's Inspector Dawson?"

He nodded toward the alley.

I rushed out to find Dawson and Mullins smoking in the alley where they were less likely to burn down the theater. "Two big men came up from the cellar a couple of minutes ago. They went in the direction of the attic."

"Good."

Chapter Twenty-Five

I looked at Inspector Dawson, speechless for a moment. "Good?"

"Just keep watch."

"And Old Nick has vanished."

"Nothing unusual there."

"If there's something interesting going on in the Regent, Old Nick is always here. You've overlooked something," I said and stormed back into the theater. The inspector was too relaxed. Was he getting a share of the proceeds from the goods? What did he know that I didn't?

I went back to the props table to find things had been moved around and something was missing. "Mr. Baker! Mr. Baker!" I whispered frantically.

"What happened here?" he asked, looking in horror at the table.

"I had to tell Inspector Dawson something and—"

"This is why you never leave the table."

"Did you see anyone here?"

"No. But that wasn't my job."

"Can you help me straighten this out?"

He quickly re-sorted the props. "The only thing you're missing is a large pair of scissors."

"I know there's a smaller pair in the props room," I said. "I'll get them."

"Here. You need the key."

I took it, opened the props storage, and quickly found the scissors. I locked up the cupboard, and on the way back, tried locking the door to the stairs leading to the cellar. It worked. Every lock seemed to use the same key, which wasn't surprising in an old building. Then I returned Mr. Baker's key to him.

"Don't leave this table again for anything."

I nodded. The police had been warned whether they wanted to be or not. Someone had stolen a lethal pair of scissors, and that someone, or someone else, was giving me grief by messing up the props table.

The rest of the second act ran smoothly. As it ended, the audience gave the actors a standing ovation as they usually did, and the actors took bow after bow. Everyone's attention was focused on the stage.

Movement behind me made me turn my head. The two large men, each carrying a cluster of large bundles, stopped at the locked cellar door. One of them pulled out an old key and unlocked it before both of them disappeared down the stairs. I rose to follow them, looking around frantically for someone to tell before I vanished into the tunnels and openings below street level.

Nora and Si were standing nearby where they were waiting for Marnie. "The black-market goods have just been carried out through the cellar. I'm going to follow them. Tell the police," I shouted over the applause.

Si looked startled, but Nora nodded.

I opened the now-unlocked door and tiptoed down the stairs. The area around the stairs was dark, but ahead of me was the front of the stage with light leaking in through the air vents. Beyond the applause coming in with the light from the audience, I heard footsteps rather than saw the men heading down a second staircase.

When I looked, I could see their torches shining ahead of them. They were headed toward Shaftsbury, where they could come up in a dozen buildings or bomb sites. I hurried as fast as I dared down the dark stairs, keeping watch on the torch beams.

Once I reached the bottom, I started out picking my way carefully toward the beams of light. After a few feet, I stopped. The torch light had disappeared. I took a few more steps in the direction where I had last seen the beams, but everything was black.

Something touched my shoulder and I jumped, shaking, without turning around. "We know where they're coming out. If they're blocked by our men that way but escape, they'll come back this way and we'll catch them." I recognized Inspector Dawson's voice whispering in my ear and sagged in relief. When I turned to face him, though, he was just a dark blob among three or four.

"I followed them this far and then lost them," I murmured in return.

"Go back upstairs. We have this now."

"I want to help."

"Go. Back. Upstairs."

Dawson made it clear I was not wanted. Using the light coming in above the stairs, I made my way in that direction until I saw someone coming down them and, for a moment, I saw a flash of light reflected off something metal.

I moved to the side and the figure passed quite close to me without realizing I was there. The fact I was holding my breath and scared into immobility may have had something to do with my invisibility.

Police whistles sounded somewhere close by. Figures ran by, aided by small torchlight beams. When they came close, Dawson and the policemen in front of me turned on their brighter torches.

Focused as they were on capturing the men in front of them, the police were not watching their rear. The dark figure ran in a crouch toward them and then I saw the flash again, up high.

"Look out!" I shouted a second before one of the figures collapsed with a moan.

Then it became a chaos of bodies thrashing around in the uncertain torchlight. One of the figures came toward me silhouetted by the faint light, his own torch turned off. Not a policeman, I guessed as I stepped out of the way.

He moved past me, apparently unaware of me. I stepped

behind him and kicked blindly, hoping to get one of his legs. I caught the back of his knee and he went down. The shiny object clattered on the cement floor.

I was grabbed from behind and I gave a shout.

"I told you to go up to the theater, Mrs. Redmond," the inspector's voice said in my ear. He flashed his torch past me and said, "Who's this?"

Old Nick lay unmoving on the floor, the scissors a foot away.

"Now I know who stole from the props table," I said. They looked odd, however. "What is that on—?"

"Blood. One of the black-market thugs was stabbed in the arm."

"Did you get all the black-market people?"

"Two of them. The other escaped, unless they picked him up at the other end. With the blackout starting soon, I'm not sure. And Old Nick came down here and attacked them. Why?"

"I thought he was part of the black-market ring. No one else could have arranged to hide the goods in the attic and keep other people out."

Figures, one in handcuffs, one clutching his arm, were helped up the first set of stairs and then continued farther up to the backstage area. "I'll take the scissors into evidence. You can take charge of moving this prisoner," the inspector said to someone. "And you," he said to me, "get upstairs where we can keep an eye on you."

I followed his directions.

* * *

After I had put away the props for the night and had everything checked by Mr. Baker, I found Si, Marnie, and Nora waiting for me. The blackout had already begun by that time.

They asked what happened and I gave an abbreviated account.

"You'll never make it home to the outskirts of London in the dark," Si said. "You can stay with Marnie. She has a large house and I'm sure it's closer than yours."

I was shocked that Si would make that offer of someone else's house. Perhaps they were better friends than I realized.

"Please do," Marnie echoed. "And I promised you an explanation. Si, come with us and tell the story."

My father had thought I might be another day at Abby's, so I saw no reason not to take her up on the offer. And I really wanted to hear the whole story.

"Are you sure?" It was Si's turn to be shocked. "Livvy's a newspaper reporter, and this would be a scoop. All her instincts will tell her to write this story."

"I can keep a secret that needs to be kept quiet," I told him. Hadn't I been trusted with our government's secrets and kept them safe? Of course, they didn't know that.

"Livvy has shown herself to be a good friend to us. We need to be honest with her so she can focus on finding Marshall's killer," Marnie said, looking into his eyes.

"I'm not going to be truly free until she does find the killer, am I? The police have no interest in solving this killing, now that one possibility has died in an accident." Si shook his head.

"Joe Landry was murdered. That was no accident," I told him. "Which leaves you in a worse position."

He put up his hands. "Whatever you want to know, just ask."

"I think we all need to head home. It's a bit of a walk, and it's not getting any brighter out there," Nora said. Si gave Marnie his arm and they led the way out the stage door and into the blackness.

Having spent quite a few evenings at the Regent, I knew we started out heading toward Oxford Street. Bomb sites were plentiful, sometimes cutting across part of the street, and with little light except for our personal torches, all of our attention was focused on the ground beneath our feet.

Nora took my arm. "I'll watch where we're stepping, you watch out for vehicles." Running with blacked-out headlamps, cars and buses were nearly upon me before I could see them coming out of the night. Once, I had to grab Si, who was walking in front of me, and pull him back before he stepped into the path of a car.

New bombings hadn't happened in a couple of months, but the bomb smell, charcoaled wooden beams and thick dust with a faint overlay of rot, hadn't left London yet.

We continued on with an occasional stumble to Oxford Street and then crossed carefully. With more vehicles and pedestrians out these days, we moved in herds while the vehicles moved slowly. Once on the other side, we went down a side street that hadn't been touched by German bombs.

I no longer had any idea where we were. Adam's and my flat hadn't been too far from there, but in the dark, with landmarks blown apart, I was completely disoriented. I followed Si and let Nora lead me.

After another few minutes of walking, we paused on the pavement. Si shined his torch into Marnie's bag while she rummaged around until she found her house key. Then she opened a gate and walked through, leading us up a single step where we waited until she unlocked the door.

Once I stumbled in, Nora shut the door behind me while Marnie pulled the curtain in the hallway aside. I kept blinking while my eyes adjusted to the light. When they did, I found I was in a Victorian hallway with a dining room to the side through an open doorway.

An older woman appeared from a staircase saying, "Supper will be in just a moment, if you'd care to go into the dining room now."

"That sounds wonderful, Agnes," Marnie said. "Is Annie joining us? There's someone I want her to meet."

"I'll see. She knows there's someone—additional here."

"Tell her Si and I are here and we'd love to have supper with her. And we'd love for her to meet our friend."

The woman smiled. "I'll tell her."

We went into the dining room off the main hall. The table, chairs, and sideboard were heavy, dark pieces of furniture left over from the Victorian age. The wallpaper was faded with smoke from decades of coal fires. They had me sit on the far side of the table at the other end.

Si sat next to me and Marnie across the table from me while Nora went downstairs. A moment later, Marnie popped up to put soup bowls at six places, then small plates, and then silverware.

"May I help?" I asked.

"Nora will send the supper up in the dumbwaiter and then she'll join us. There's nothing for you to do. Just relax, Livvy," Si said. A moment later, the lift from the kitchen groaned into position and Si carried over the meal to set it on the table.

By that time, Nora had joined us. "She's coming," she said, sounding equal measures pleased and relieved.

I didn't know what to expect. Queen Victoria? Sarah Bernhardt? Gracie Fields?

After a minute, Agnes came into the room alone. She turned back and said to someone standing behind the wall, "Come along, child. Supper is on the table and Mummy and Daddy are here."

Mummy? Daddy? All the women here, except me, were past childbearing age. A grandchild, left behind in the bombing raids? A young child was the last thing I had expected the mystery person to be.

I stared at the door waiting for my questions to be answered. Wondering who this person was, and if they had anything to do with Si's willingness to go to jail rather than admit to this secret.

Chapter Twenty-Six

Then a small figure peeped around the doorframe. Not a child, a short adult. An adult perhaps older than me. With a ribbon in her brown hair and carrying a teddy bear.

"This is Annie," Marnie said. "My daughter."

"Our daughter," Si added.

I smiled at her. "Hello, Annie. I'm Livvy." She had the smooth skin of someone who never worried and the unformed features of someone who would never grow up. Her dumpy body was encased in a housedress.

"Hi, Livvy." She smiled back. Marnie scooted down across the table from me and Annie sat down at the table across from Si.

We had a tasty potato and leek soup with thinly sliced, slightly stale bread. I noticed Annie was the only one to have jam with her bread.

Our dinner conversation was kept on neutral subjects, how that night's performance went, the latest rationing guidelines, and the bluebirds Annie had seen in the park that day. The potato and leek soup was delicious, and I thanked them for sharing such a good meal with me.

After dinner, Agnes took Annie upstairs to ready her for

bed. Si promised to read her a bedtime story before he left.

I raised my eyebrows at Marnie and she nodded.

Nora put the dishes on the lift and went out of the room.

"The year I didn't work in the theater, when I was supposedly banned by my husband, Marshall Lowe, I was really having Annie," Marnie told me. "You don't think we're strange for not putting her in a home?"

I quickly figured Annie had been born before the Great War and was about my age. "No. Not if you don't want to. She doesn't seem to be any trouble. Agnes takes care of her when you need to be at the theater?"

"Yes, Agnes has been with us nearly ten years. She's a godsend. She cooks and watches Annie and we have dailies come in to do the cleaning. When I have to go on tour, Agnes is in charge of the house." Marnie smiled at Si. "And Si is always in town."

"I owe you an apology for misdirecting you on Marnie's motives for killing Lowe. It was the only thing I could think of on the spur of the moment and since it was Marnie's choice at that time not to tell you, there was nothing for me to say. I'm sorry," Si said.

"It wasn't a wise choice, but apology accepted. I understand your desire to keep the truth hidden," I said. Most people in the days before the Great War put afflicted children away in facilities. Lunatic asylums. Marnie was very forward thinking in keeping Annie at home.

"Before you ask, Annie is my daughter, not Lowe's. After Annie was born, when we could have wed, Marnie refused to consider it. She didn't want any more children," Si told me.

"And I need to keep Annie well away from the limelight. Can you imagine the hateful things reporters would say if they knew about her?" Marnie stared at me. "Please don't tell anyone."

"I wouldn't. Do the police know?"

"No." Marnie looked horrified.

"They may have to be told. They think whatever Si is hiding is some longstanding hatred of Marshall Lowe. Since Si is Annie's father, that only works the other way around as a motive."

"You see, Annie is my alibi," Si said. "Agnes needed to go out that evening, so I watched Annie, read her stories, entertained her while Lowe was being poisoned. I can't tell the police that, not without revealing Annie's existence. Neither Marnie nor I want her questioned by the police. Hounded by the press."

"I can understand that. And I'm sorry I pressed you for an answer." Then I looked at Si. "Agnes didn't kill him, did she?"

Marnie laughed. "She's never even met Marshall."

"That's good, then." Then I asked Si, "Why did you never work in the theater again?"

"I was rubbish as an actor, but I was a decent reporter." He shook his head. "Lowe could never again tell me how bad I was in any role. I could, however, report on how terrible he was as a director to thousands of people."

"Again, the motive is the wrong way around." Then I

looked sharply at Marnie. "Unless Marshall Lowe was threatening to tell everyone about Annie."

"No. Why would he? He could have done that any time in the last thirty years. In fact, he was glad to divorce me so he didn't have anything to do with the child even before she was born. He was grateful to get out of our marriage and not have to pay me anything."

"I really don't think we need to explain all this to the police," Si said.

"Did Joe Landry know about Annie?" I asked.

"How could he?" Marnie asked. "We are the only ones who do, besides Nora and Marshall."

"Then why would he, or Bert Lanshire if he was the target the second time, be killed?"

"I have no idea. Joe was a harmless, sweet boy. I've worked with Bert before and he's a nice, quiet man with grandchildren who've been sent to the countryside."

"Neither one would hurt a fly," Si added.

"The scenery rope was cut. Someone wanted to kill someone," I exclaimed in frustration.

"Who else was standing there when the rope gave way?" Si asked.

"I was getting ready to go onstage and was back a distance from the scenery," Marnie said. "As were you, Livvy. The only person the killer could have confidently expected to hit with the falling scenery was Joe. He was pulling down on the rope. That Bert was there was due to a mix-up."

"Bud Cosby could easily have been killed if Robbie Day

hadn't pulled him out of the way in time. Which means it probably wasn't Day who cut the rope," I said.

"Well, it wasn't Joe or Bert. Or Old Nick, come to that," Si said.

"Why not?" I was sure about Joe or Bert, but not the crazy old man.

"Old Nick was Joe's uncle. Got Joe the job and everything. And they were the only ones left in their family."

"Did a bomb finish the rest of them off?"

"No. Some tragedy years ago," Si said with a shrug. There seemed to be a lot of that.

"This isn't getting any of us to bed," Marnie said around a yawn. "I can lend you a nightgown and Agnes will have made up the guest room for you."

"I need to read a bedtime story," Si said and rose. He kissed Marnie on the top of her head and left, Marnie and me following more slowly.

* * *

After a good night's sleep with a decent breeze coming in the window, I woke up refreshed and slightly bewildered in a strange bed. It took me only a moment to remember where I was and where I needed to go that morning.

And that led to what I would have to tell my father. My mood sank.

I came downstairs for a breakfast of weak coffee and dry toast. Annie was just finishing, and the two of us carried on a short, polite conversation. Agnes put the lid on Annie's jam jar, making it clear whose it was.

I heard the front door unlock and then Si came in, helping himself to toast and coffee. "What are you doing today? Working for the police, the Regent Theatre, or *The Stage?*"

"*The Stage.* I need to make some telephone calls from the office. Then I'll go over to the theater."

"I'll see you one place or the other," he replied. "Oh, wait. It's Thursday. Do you want me to take this week's issue to the printer's this morning?"

"That would make my day easier if you would." Especially in light of what I had planned. Just thinking about what the future held frightened me.

Once I finished my breakfast, Marnie came into the dining room. I thanked her for her hospitality, told her I'd see her at the theater, and left.

I went into *The Stage* offices. From there I phoned for a doctor's appointment before Mr. Bridges or Si arrived. As they put it, they kept theater hours.

It was nice having the office to myself in the morning. And while I appreciated the quiet to try to piece together the mystery of the two deaths at the Regent Theatre, I was no further forward when they arrived. I told them goodbye and left since it was time for me to see the doctor.

The doctor's appointment was one I'd prefer to forget. I had no idea what to expect. The doctor himself was of average height and build, with thinning light brown hair and glasses. After a short examination while the nurse handed him things I couldn't see past the screen, the doctor quickly told me that I was expecting, probably late February, and the various changes I would experience to my body. He was matter-of-fact, since he'd been through this a thousand times. I shivered.

After I dressed, I went into his office, where he signed standard notes directing the authorities to give me more food rations up to and after giving birth and more clothing coupons for my expanding body and for my baby's layette.

I left in a state of shock, clutching my bag to me with the notes from the doctor inside. Now that I was certain, I'd have to tell my father, but I had no idea how he would react. I knew it wouldn't be pretty.

But I was looking forward to telling Adam. Perhaps for news as monumental as this, he might get more leave. He might even be able to find quarters for us now.

If not, I'd have to bring a baby into my father's house, and he would not be pleased.

I couldn't wait to tell Abby that she was correct. And Esther would be overjoyed by the news as well. I wished my mother had lived to see this day, but then my father—how would my father have reacted to my news if my mother was still with us?

Suddenly, I discovered I'd walked the whole way to the *Daily Premier* building. I supposed I needed to tell Sir Henry. He was my boss, and obviously pregnant women weren't allowed to work, no matter how many men we were replacing who had gone into the army.

I went upstairs, where his secretary had me wait until a

delegation from the printers left Sir Henry's office. Then she sent me in.

I sat in a chair facing his desk and blurted out my news. No "Good morning." No "I have news of a personal nature." And then I watched as Sir Henry grinned at me as if he was the proud father. Or grandfather.

"I'm very happy for you," he said. "When will the baby arrive?"

"Late February."

"You can work well into the autumn, if you want."

"I want to."

"Good. How is your current assignment coming?"

I sighed and leaned back in my chair. "I know what Si has been hiding, and I've told him to tell the police. His secret is more a reason for Marshall Lowe to kill him than the other way around. But nothing is telling me who did kill the director."

"What about the stagehand who was killed by falling scenery? Just an accident, do you think?"

"No. The rope had been cut, sending down the scenery and the sandbag. And the stagehand was the only one who should have been in the area when it fell."

Sir Henry scowled. "Are the two murders related?"

"Different methods, different days. Lowe's murder was planned and should have been error-free. The method of the stagehand's death could have missed, could have killed someone else, did hurt the props man."

"One was careful, the other reckless," Sir Henry said.

"Sounds as if you have two different killers."

I shook my head. "In one small theater? A theater that has already had black-market goods hidden away in the attic. And a suicide over the script."

"Who was involved in whatever happened to the script to drive someone to kill himself?" Sir Henry scowled as he considered our mystery.

"Marshall Lowe, mainly, changed the play to a form that the playwright, Philip Bernard, couldn't stand. And now Bud Cosby, the new director, has made more changes, but this was after the playwright died."

"And this script led to Bernard's suicide? Could this unfortunate have been killed by a family member or close friend rather than do this to himself?"

"The author of the original play had his mother murdered by his grandmother, who subsequently was discovered to have killed the grandfather as well. The uncle had already been hanged for the crime when they finally figured out it was the grandmother. The author had no siblings, nor was he married. There is no one else. Maybe being so alone in the world led the author to suicide."

"What about the author's father or his family?"

"He was long gone, and no one knows about any family on that side," I told him.

"Might be worth checking up on. You might want to go into the archives and find out what we have on the case. It's been more than ten years, but I vaguely remember we covered Mrs. Bernard's murder, the trial, and then the finding of the body and the second trial. Look it up," Sir Henry said. "I'm not surprised the police haven't been through the archives, but they have all their official records."

"I should have started there, but since Philip Bernard died a day before Marshall Lowe, and he seemed so addled, it seemed as if there couldn't be a connection. There might be one. Thank you." I rose and hurried from the office downstairs to the newspaper morgue, the archives where the stories could be found.

With the help of one of the women currently working in the file room, we finally found the murder of Velma Bernard fifteen years before. Philip lost his mother at such a young age. No wonder he was so protective of his script and, once he had sold it to Marshall Lowe, angry at how his story was warped beyond recognition.

I turned pages in the binder holding the editions for that year until I found the edition of the day after the murder. There was a photo of a pale, thin young woman, no doubt overworked, standing between her large, aggressive-looking mother and her dark, thin, frightened-looking son.

As I stared at the photo of the boy, he seemed to stare back at me with wide eyes. I changed my opinion from frightened to terrified.

The original article mentioned that the body of Velma Bernard was found brutally murdered not far from her house. Her purse was missing. The next day's article mentioned she was last seen with her brother George, a ne'er-do-well with a record for petty theft.

I continued reading, stopping when I finally focused on the man's full name. George Landry. Was Joe a relative of his? He'd have only been a baby when this murder and George's subsequent arrest occurred. And Landry was a common name.

I wished I'd had the sense to read the clippings before Joe Landry was killed.

Chapter Twenty-Seven

I kept reading the articles on the murder and then about the trial held a little over two months later. Rose Landry, George's mother, was quoted in the newspaper. Knowing that she had later been convicted of killing her daughter and her husband, I was suspicious of anything she said. So far, I'd not stumbled on a motive.

The same as Marshall Lowe's murder.

It was a shame I hadn't been able to find a copy of Philip Bernard's play. With any luck, it might have given us a clue as to why Lowe was murdered. It would hopefully have told me more about the people I was reading about in the newspaper articles.

The trial had lasted less than two full days. George Landry, with his criminal record, was quickly found guilty by the jury and sentenced to hang. I looked ahead and found a short notice that George Landry had been hanged in prison. None of his family had attended. Then it mentioned he had left behind two children. There was no mention of a wife.

Had she still been alive? Were they not married? Was one of the children Joe? Who was the other one?

I went back to the original murder edition and read

slowly forward, but I found no clues as to the identities of the two children or whether George had ever been married. I did see a byline on the stories that I recognized. I went to find him.

Back upstairs in the newsroom, I found P. L. Gray at his usual desk, chewing on an unlit cigar and writing. He had a round face and a round belly despite the rationing that had made the rest of us thinner.

"Gray," I said, "can I ask you about a trial you covered about fifteen years ago?"

"Yeah. Let me find the right notebook." He began banging the drawers in his desk, flipping through notebooks and grunting until he found what he wanted. "Which trial?"

"George Landry murder trial for killing his sister."

"Oh, yeah. Didn't they decide later he didn't do it? His mother did it?"

I nodded.

He started flipping through notebooks until he came to the right case. "What do you need?"

"Did you ever find his wife or his children?"

"She wasn't his wife. They'd been living together for years, but he'd never married her. At that point, she was grateful he hadn't. She wanted nothing to do with his family, especially his mother, and the old lady hated her."

"What was the not-wife's name?"

He flipped forward and backward in his notebook a few pages. "Here it is. Blanche. Blanche Everett. She was a dancer, worked in variety shows."

"Does she still? Is she still alive?" I hoped he knew a little more about her.

"Have no idea. I haven't seen her since the trial. I know she didn't attend the hanging."

"You said George's mother didn't like her. That feeling was mutual?"

"Oh, yes. There was one instance in the lobby outside the courtroom when we broke for midday that I saw for myself. The grandmother, Rose, who was more of a thorn than anything, told Blanche she'd take her children away from her. Since she was a dancer in 'those filthy shows,' as she called them, Rose knew she could get the courts to give them to her. Blanche asked her if she'd raise them to be killers the way she had their father. I thought they'd come to blows."

"Did they? What happened?"

"George's solicitor took Blanche by the arm and led her out of the building, away from Rose. But from the looks those two women gave each other I'd say they were both ready to kill the other."

"Would George's solicitor have any information on Blanche or the children?"

"He might. Why?" Gray looked at me as if I was a rival newspaper reporter searching for the key to my story in his notes.

"Sir Henry has me trying to find the killer of the director Marshall Lowe. The number one suspect, Si Chapell, is an old friend of his. And once I ruled out everything else around that theater, I was left with the play. A play originally written by Velma Bernard's son about his mother's murder that Marshall Lowe bought and rewrote as a comedy."

"A comedy? There was nothing remotely funny about that family." Gray nearly dropped his cigar.

"Lowe changed a great deal. I suspect nothing remains of the original play that he bought, but I've not been able to find a copy of the original play."

"You think the playwright killed him?"

"Philip Bernard killed himself a day before Lowe's death apparently in despair over what Marshall Lowe had done to his work and his realization that the original would probably never see the light of day."

"Then why are you interested in George's family?"

"They may not have avenged Bernard's suicide on Lowe, or tried to get the original play away from him, but on the other hand, they may have."

He wrote something on a piece of paper and handed it to me. "George's solicitor's name and address. Mind, it is fifteen years old. Possibly more."

I went to the telephone directories and checked. There was no listing for Blanche Everett. There was for the solicitor, so I called the number and made an appointment for that afternoon. I was glad there wasn't a matinee that day, since I was still the temporary props man.

After stopping at a luncheon place that had popped up since rationing and the Blitz had changed the landscape, and having a meal of soup and stale bread, I went out to the northern part of London, where they'd escaped most of the bombing. The solicitor's office was in a former dress shop, if the faded lettering between the ground and first floors could be believed. The solicitor's firm's name was painted in new paint on the door.

I walked in and found myself in a small lobby facing the receptionist's desk. I gave my name and stated my business and was told to have a seat and wait. I took a chair with a leather seat held in place with brass rivets and looked around. Very old law books sat behind glass doors in shelves, but still gave the fairly new building an ancient, musty odor.

After a few minutes, I was called to an office in the back of the building that had one large desk surrounded along the walls with filing cabinets. The man standing behind the desk as I was ushered in was tall, lean, and middle-aged. Despite the heat, he wore a dark suit and waistcoat of heavy wool with a high, white shirt collar.

"Please sit down, Mrs. Redmond," he said in a deep funereal voice. "How may I help you?"

"I'm looking for the companion and children of a client of yours about fifteen years ago. A man named George Landry."

"That was a long time ago. What is your interest in finding them now?"

"There is a play running in the West End called *Have You Seen My Mother-in-Law*? The play originally was written by Philip Bernard, son of Velma Bernard, and based on the household he grew up in. One of the stagehands was killed in an accident on stage. His name was Joe Landry, and I think he might be George Landry's son."

"If he were George's son, he would be a first cousin to this Philip Bernard."

"Yes." I had figured that much out. It wasn't difficult.

"I will have to consult old files to find out if this stagehand is indeed George's son. How old is he?"

"He was about eighteen. Any older and he would have been conscripted into the service." Then I turned the tables. "He was one of two siblings. Was he the older or the younger?"

"Again, I'll have to consult my files." The solicitor was jotting down notes.

"Do you have the address for Blanche Everett, George's love interest?"

"I doubt it will be current, but I can check."

"Thank you. When will you have any information on Miss Everett or the two children available for me?"

"I'm not certain I'll be able to release any information to you. Not without their approval."

"And if you find they are dead? They won't be giving you approval then."

"I doubt we'd know if they are dead. It's been fifteen years or more. They may have changed their names. Left the country. Anything may have happened to them."

"Then I doubt you will be reneging your responsibilities by giving me fifteen-year-old information."

"We'll see. Come back at ten tomorrow and I'll see what

we can release to you."

* * *

I learned nothing working at the props table at the Regent Theatre that night. As soon as the show was over, I picked up the props, stored them in the props cupboard, and headed home. It was growing dark when I unlocked the door and entered my father's house.

He was in his study, reading. "You have a letter from Adam," he said by way of greeting as he slid it toward the edge of his desk with one finger.

I quickly opened it and read the familiar script. Now was the time to tell my father the news he was least likely to appreciate, short of the Germans have invaded. "He'll be here next weekend…"

"Oh, that's good news."

"And it will be the perfect opportunity to tell him about the baby."

"What baby?" came out cautiously, as if his words were defusing an unexploded bomb.

"Our baby."

That jerked his attention away from his book. "Good Lord. Are you planning on raising it in this house?" His voice rose to the rafters.

"Until the war ends and the country can rebuild the housing we need, I have no choice."

"But babies are loud. And messy." He actually shuddered at the thought of his grandchild.

"Then what do you propose?"

"Move in with Adam."

"We've talked about that. There is no housing at all anywhere within twenty miles of where he is stationed."

"I'm sure Abby would love to have a baby in the house again."

"She took in two orphans. That's more than enough to ask of her and Sir John."

"What about Esther?"

"What about Esther?" I was barely keeping from snapping at him.

"You said Sir Henry bought her a big house and there's a room for you to stay in when you visit. She has a cook and a nursery maid and daily help. Sounds as if it is the perfect place for you to bring up your baby until the war ends and Adam comes home."

"'Visit.' Surely that's the important word there. I can't afford a nursery maid, if there was even one available to hire. And in a few months, I'll be out of a job. Then we'll only have Adam's salary, and that won't go very far."

My father sighed. "We won't solve this tonight, and I'm sure we'll have a few months to come up with a good solution." He hesitated and then said, "Congratulations. Is it a boy?"

"You'd want that, wouldn't you? I don't know. That's something else we'll just have to wait and see."

"Olivia, you know I've always wished you had been a boy, but that was because once your mother died, I was out of my element." He smiled contentedly. "Your mother would have handled a grandchild in the house much better than I would. But I know you and Adam will be excellent parents."

"Thank you." I tried to return a smile. While I understood he would never welcome a newborn in his house disrupting his rigid schedule, I wished he could have sounded happier for us.

At least he was trying to say the right words.

Then I remembered Annie and wondered if Marnie Keller had been as happy as I was now before her baby was born. I had no idea what I would get. Boy, girl, normal, disabled.

I was sure I would love my child. I was equally sure my father wouldn't, no matter how perfect the baby was.

My father broke into my thoughts. "Mrs. Johnson will be happy to hear about your change in fortune. She's been wondering how long it would be before this happened."

"That's nice to hear. I hope she doesn't mind having Adam here next weekend."

"I'm sure she'll be as glad to see him as I will be."

I almost burst out laughing. No one was ever as happy to see Adam as my father was. Adam was the son he never had. If Adam made my father the grandfather to a grandson, he would assume deity status.

Whereas I would continue to be irrelevant.

Chapter Twenty-Eight

The next day, after an unusual lack of silence over coffee and toast thanks to Mrs. Johnson, I made my way northeast on the Underground until I reached the office of the solicitor who might tell me what I needed to know. Then again, he said he might not, even if he had the information.

It was too hot to dress in a business suit, even in a thin wool. Instead, I chose a cotton-linen blend dress in a pale green without a belt and hoped the solicitor would take pity on me.

I was taken into his office on time and told to sit. Then he opened a large folder and said, "Blanche Everett died five years ago. She was buried in a large cemetery north of here. I have the details here."

"And the children?"

"Still alive, as far as I know. Joseph Landry would be about eighteen years old now. I have his address here. Carol Landry would be about twenty-three. I have her address also. These details are from the time of reading the mother's will."

I rose. "Joe Landry was killed last week."

"If it's the same man," the solicitor reminded me.

"I think it is," I told him, taking the single typed sheet he gave me. "Thank you."

I left the office and headed toward the address given for Joe. The entire end of the street in the East End was nothing but damaged homes and rubble, just as Joe had said.

I had lunch in the area and then went to the Regent Theatre before the matinee, my mind working on where I could live once the baby was born. Mrs. Johnson had been happy for me and told my father that the baby and I should come back to his house from the lying-in hospital and stay there for six weeks with the aid of a part-time nurse. It would be criminal to do otherwise. She said it in a tone that for once made my father sit up and take notice.

Even if he let the baby and me stay for six weeks, where would I go after that?

I was idly rearranging the props table when I suddenly realized someone was saying my name in my ear. I jumped and turned to face him.

Gil Baker said, "You were a million miles away. Is everything all right?"

"No, but it will be. What can I do for you?" I managed a smile for him.

"Bert Lanshire's foot is healing nicely, and he'll be ready to come back to work in about a week for seated work only."

"I'm glad to hear it. And I'm sure Bert is too."

"What will you do?"

"Go back to being a reporter." It was the job I'd always wanted.

"What about our killer? We've had two deaths." Gil Baker seemed anxious that we find the guilty party after so much death and destruction.

"I know. And unless someone is willing to tell me or the police something useful, I don't think it will ever be solved."

"How long will your boss allow you to hang around here?"

"That's not the problem. I'm carrying a child, and once I start showing, I'm out of here."

A broad grin crossed his face. "That's great. Best wishes to you and the little one. Father in the army?"

"Yes. Off training, so he's not around much." My smile was a little wobbly.

"Well, we'll make sure no one disturbs you around here."

"Why is that?" Si asked as he came from the direction of Marnie's dressing room.

"Your reporter is carrying a little one," Gil told him.

I could feel my face heat.

"Why, that's wonderful. Have you told Sir Henry?"

"Yes."

My tone silenced both men. Gil immediately found he needed to be elsewhere doing anything else. Si looked as if he wanted to pat my shoulder. It was Marnie, coming up to join us, who saved the day.

Si whispered in her ear and she smiled from one ear to the other. "I thought so. You've been positively glowing."

"I don't know about—"

"Positively glowing," she interrupted. "Have you been in touch with your soldier boy?"

"No, but he has leave for next weekend, so I will be able to tell him in person."

"Oh, that's wonderful. All you have to do now is solve our little problem."

"What?" I felt my eyes widen.

"We need our killer caught." She held my gaze.

"Then the actors are going to have to tell me the truth."

"Oh, they will, I'll make sure of it, or my name's not Harriet Girtbottom."

"Excuse me?" I was now staring at her, open-mouthed.

"Harriet Girtbottom. That's my real name."

"I thought that only movie stars changed their names," I said. Was someone else here under an assumed name, killing people associated with this play?

"Oh, no. Lots of us do it," Marnie assured me.

"What was Marshall Lowe's real name? What was yours, Si?"

"It was Marshall Lowe, and Si's is Simon Chapell," Marnie said.

"It's only names that are awful that are changed. Or too close to someone else's name," Si told me.

"How would I find out actors' real names?"

"You could ask them," Si said.

"Or Ian Nelson. The producer needs to pay the cast and crew," Marnie told me.

"Do you know where he is?"

"In his office. But hurry. Curtain up in twenty," Marnie said before she rushed off in the other direction to her dressing room.

I found Nelson poring over ledgers in his cramped office. I squeezed in past the file cabinet and the shelves and said, "Excuse me, but do you know which actors use pseudonyms?"

He looked up at me, blinked, and took off his wire-rimmed spectacles. "You mean, stage names? No. Whatever name they tell me, I put on the books. Their agents might know. Why?"

"It's probably nothing." I went backstage using the hallways unseen by the audience. Near the stage door, I ran into Diana Carroll and Jane Barber. "Are your stage names your real names?"

"I'm late. I don't have time for pretend detectives," Diana said and rushed past me.

Jane walked past me and turned around. "None of your business," she told me with a cheeky grin and then kept going.

I glanced at the clock and found I didn't have any time for these questions either.

Mercifully, no one was killed at that afternoon's performance and no props disappeared. I left the table ready for the evening performance and hurried after Gloria Snelling, the first daughter, and Bud Cosby, our actor director. "Do either of you use stage names?"

Cosby laughed. "I wasn't christened Bud, if that's what

you're asking. I'm 'Frederick Hannibal Cosby' on my birth certificate."

"I wasn't named 'Gloria Snelling,' but I'm not going to admit to my name."

"Why not?"

"Because it's horrid."

"Surely not as bad as 'Harriet Girtbottom,'" Cosby said with another laugh.

"But close. And don't you say a word," Gloria said with a shake of her pointer finger. She looped her arm around Cosby's, and they headed out through the stage door.

"Getting some dinner?" Gil asked as he and the stagehands walked past.

"Yes. Please," I answered, and I walked a short distance with them, eventually stopping at a local pub that had a restaurant in the back. We all had fish and chips and canned peas and washed it down with weak beer or tea.

"How many of the actors use made-up names rather than their own?" I asked Gil who was sitting next to me.

"Don't they all?" he replied.

"Do you know any of their real names?"

He shook his head. "It would be too much to keep track of. You see, I don't care. Actors come and go in a theater. Another week, another play, another group of actors. It's all the same to me."

"Even if it might explain who the murderer is?"

"How could it do that?"

"I'm looking for a Carol Landry, who is Joe's sister. It's

possible she's working at the Regent and she may know what happened to her brother."

He shrugged. "Who might it be?"

"Any of the three sisters in the play. Or Wanda Thomas, who played a sister in the play for the entire tour until it came to the Regent. Or the young costumer, Millie."

"Oh, my daughter knows her. Her name's been Millie for several years, at least." Gil finished his chips and his peas in one bite.

"Carol Landry could have changed her name as much as fifteen years ago."

Gil sat quietly for a minute, chewing. "And she'd only been a child then."

"Yes."

"What was the mother's maiden name?"

"Everett."

"Maybe the mother changed their names."

"Then why didn't she change Joe's?" I asked.

"Well, you know it can't be the girl who broke her leg. Wanda, was that her name?"

"Why?"

"The tacks were taken out of the rug. I saw that. It was sabotage. And it removed her from the cast. Someone who wanted to kill Marshall Lowe would have wanted to stay in the cast, make it easier to find her chance to murder him."

Gil shrugged as he rose and put his money on the table with the other men's. I set my fork down, since the fish stank and most of what I could keep down was chips. I put my money down as I rushed to follow them.

"Gil, you're brilliant," I told him as I caught up.

We returned to the theater in time to set up for the evening performance. The auditorium was already filling with members of the audience, half in uniform and half in evening dress. When I had a free minute, I dashed to the open space in the back of the stage and whispered "Carol" from behind the two costumers.

Both of them lifted their heads to look around and then went back to work sewing.

I tried it a second time, a little louder.

This time neither of them reacted in any way. I suspected neither Millie nor the other costumer were Carol Landry.

I went back to the props table, trying to keep a close watch on Marnie's three stage daughters. At the end of the evening performance, I was nowhere closer to figuring out who the killer was than I was before.

Unless—could it really be that simple?

* * *

I had recognized the address for Carol Landry as being in the Covent Garden area. When I arrived there the next day, I found the entire street was intact, untouched by the bombing. The building I wanted contained offices, including a theatrical agent's office. Since the murders had taken place in a theater, I started there.

The secretary was beautiful, with delicate bone structure, milky skin, blond hair, big, blue eyes, and a light hand with makeup. But her voice, when she called out "Mr.

Lewis," hurt down to my fingernails.

Mr. Lewis was short, bald, and loud. And direct. "Did you bring a photo with you?" he asked as he came out of his office.

"No."

"I can't do anything for you without a photo. Any experience?" He sat down behind his desk. Apparently, my name was not the first thing he needed.

I shook my head. "As a reporter? Years."

"Why didn't you say so? Who are you writing about?"

"Carol Landry."

He scowled. "That doesn't sound as if it is anyone on my books."

"She performs under another name."

"Oh. Why didn't you say so?" He rose again and opened up a file drawer. "Landry...Landry...Landry...Here we are." He pulled out a file and extracted the photo. "This her?"

It certainly was. "Diana Carroll."

"What's the story? Will it bring her fame and bigger roles?"

I couldn't tell him what I suspected. "Possibly."

Next, I traveled to Scotland Yard, but D.I. Dawson and Sergeant Mullins were out on another case. I left them a note telling them what I had learned and went on to the theater.

It was early, the crew was out to lunch and the actors hadn't arrived yet for the matinee. I was surprised that the door was unlocked, but then it occurred to me that the constable assigned duty of watching over the theater, since there had been two murders and a black-market ring operating out of there, must be around somewhere.

I tiptoed in, trying not to make any sound in case anyone else was there. The boards in the backstage area didn't squeak since no one wanted their performance ruined by someone stepping on a loose board.

Silently, I crossed to the far side, listening for voices, when I finally heard a woman's voice come from the area of the women's dressing rooms. She wasn't trying to keep her voice down, so I only had to move a little toward the back of the theater before I could make out what she was saying.

"You don't trust me, do you?" the woman's voice said in theater-trained tones.

"How can I? I remember your granny. You're her, only worse," a man's voice said, rougher and a little gaspy.

"Not at all. She was content being poor, while I'm after all the money I can get."

"Including Phil's money for the play."

"He can't use it anymore."

"Why should you have it?"

There was a pause, and then the woman said, "Ssh. I thought I heard someone."

"Just your guilty conscience."

The woman continued. "I'm not the same as my grandmother. From what my mother said, she was a right old cow."

"She was a cold-blooded killer and you're just the same."

"How dare you?"

"You killed your own brother."

The woman was Diana Carroll, also known as Carol Landry, granddaughter of Rose Landry. But why did she kill her brother, Joe? And who was she talking to?

"Idiot was in the wrong place. I was aiming for Bud Cosby."

A groan behind me made me turn toward the stage. I'd taken a few steps toward the sound when I heard a woman behind me say, "What are you doing here this early?"

Chapter Twenty-Nine

I stepped around the scenery onto the stage and immediately saw a man in a constable's uniform sprawled on the floor, blood oozing from the top of his head and his helmet several feet away. His groans told me he was regaining consciousness. I stepped to the other side of him and turned back to face Diana Carroll. Also known as Carol Landry. I was surprised to see the man with her was Old Nick.

The stage doorman looked ill, too ill to defend anyone against Carol Landry. I decided to pretend I'd just arrived.

"We need to contact the police and a doctor. This constable is seriously injured."

"What happened? Did the scenery fall on him?" Diana Carroll asked in her carrying voice.

I knelt next to him, slipping his whistle into the palm of my hand as I examined him. Then I scrambled up from the floor. "I'm not sure how he was injured."

In that short time, Diana—as I still thought of her—had closed the gap between us. In one hand she held the scissors that had gone missing from my props table once before when Old Nick had taken them.

"Did he get hit with those?" I asked, knowing the wound

wasn't the right shape.

"You know very well he didn't. Did you hear us talking?"

At that moment, a thud made us both look at Old Nick, who had collapsed.

"He looks ill," I said, for lack of anything better to say as I watched the scissors in her hand.

"It's all the drinking he does." She didn't look very concerned.

"Have you known him long?"

"Yes. He's my uncle. He's always been a drinker."

And he really was Joe's uncle, more evidence that Diana was Carol Landry. "It was a good thing he was here when Wanda Thomas broke her leg so you could snag her role."

"Had you never suspected that I took out the tacks holding the rug down? How convenient it was that I was available to take her place?" She darted around the prone constable, toward me.

I backed up. "Why would you? Did you want to work with your uncle that badly?"

"Don't be so naïve." She took another step toward me as I backed up some more.

A moan from Old Nick grabbed my attention for a moment, and that was all it took for Diana to reach me, the sharp tips of the scissors pressed into my side.

"I'm no threat to you. Just leave. I'll get help for the constable and Old Nick."

"You know too much. Move." She jabbed the scissors against me.

"I don't know anything."

"You're a fool if you think I believe that."

"What have you done? And why?" I hoped to get her talking and delay her stabbing me until help arrived. When hopefully she wouldn't get the chance.

"My cousin Philip wrote a brilliant play. He didn't realize how brilliant. He sold it to Marshall Lowe for a tidy little sum, and I planned to relieve him of the money."

"Steal it?" I asked, surprised.

"If you prefer."

"But Philip killed himself because Marshall rewrote the play and turned it into a comedy. Unless he knew you stole his money. Did you?"

"Nonsense," Diana said. "Marshall had already written the comedy. He bought Philip's tragedy because he knew how popular it would be after the war ended, when the country went on an angst fest. A mother killing her own children. A true story. Dynamite after the war. The only successes now, while things are so dire, are comedies."

"Did Philip not understand his play would be put on later?"

"We all told him that, but he didn't pay any attention. He was as daft as the rest of the family. They're all crazy."

Her family, too, but I wasn't going to point that out. "Did you find where Philip hid the money?" I asked.

"No. And I've looked everywhere. But there shouldn't be any trouble about it, since I'm the only one left to inherit."

"What about your uncle Nick? Shouldn't he inherit,

too?"

"If he lives that long."

Maybe I'd be able to use that. "Did you get the play back?"

"Not yet. Bud will put it on after the war if I can get my hands on it."

"So, you had no reason to kill Marshall Lowe," I suggested.

"I wasn't going to pay him for the play. And certainly not as much as he wanted for it. Of course, I had to kill him when he found me searching his things for it. He was going to call the police after the performance that night. He guessed I was the one who'd already searched his flat and got rid of the carpet tacks."

"What about the ripped costumes and stolen good-luck charms?"

"Oh, that was Cousin Philip. He was as batty as the rest of the family." She kept referring to the family all being batty, not realizing she sounded the same as the others.

"And Joe?"

"My brother was simple. He believed you should always tell the truth. He was going to tell the police what I'd done. Silly boy. He didn't see I did it for the two of us. He needed the money as badly as I did." She shook her head as she heard footsteps in the backstage area. "Move. Downstairs," she hissed.

She forced me over to the stairs and down into the cellar, poking me with the long, sharp scissors when I didn't move fast enough. I went down the stairs first, feeling the cool, damp air on my face.

"Why did you strike the constable?" I didn't lower my voice, hoping someone heard me.

Diana lowered hers as she replied, "He saw me going through Bud's things that he took from Marshall when he began directing our play. I suppose I could have told the constable some lie, but it seemed easier to just clobber him."

"And Old Nick?" I raised my voice slightly and felt a sharp poke in my ribs. "Ouch!"

"Will you be quiet," Diana hissed. "You do know he's Nicholas Bernard, Philip's useless father. I think he's finally drunk himself to death. Unless he's just passed out again."

The father who was missing or dead when the mother was murdered. Poor Philip. But it explained how the son was able to gain access to the theater. "You didn't poison him?"

"Why would I?" She'd forced me down the second staircase to the basement passage area, where she hesitated as if unsure in which direction to take me. "My grandmother was right. He was a useless sod."

It was dark enough in the lower level that I could barely see her face. "Your grandmother, who killed her own daughter and let your father hang for her crime? Her own child?"

I couldn't see any change of expression as she said, "You have to look out for yourself first."

"But you haven't found your cousin's copy of his play, have you? Or Marshall's?"

"No, and I can't find what my dear cousin did with the money." She sounded disgusted.

"Wait. I think I know where the money is." A place where his father would be the most likely person to find it.

"Where?" The scissors cut into my side again, this time more forcefully than before.

I shivered, cold for the first time in weeks. "Once I tell you, you'll kill me. Why should I tell you?"

"If you don't tell me, I'll kill you and take my chances."

"You'd do better to put down the scissors and come with me. Then you can take the money and leave."

"Lead the way." She didn't put down the scissors, but she held them down, no longer stabbing me in the side. It hurt, nonetheless.

I climbed the bottom run of stairs and then walked over to the upper staircase leading to the stage level. I could hear the stage level was now occupied with stagehands, actors, and hopefully the police. It was growing harder to climb the stairs, but I'd nearly reached the door at the top of the second set of stairs when I felt the scissors in my side again and heard Diana whisper, "Don't try anything or you'll be dead before you hit the ground."

I nodded, not trusting my voice not to squeak. Despite the damp chill, I was starting to sweat.

"Where's the money?"

"Follow me." I reached the door handle and opened it. No one was close enough to see what Diana held in her hand. I hoped my guess was right. I doubted I'd live to make a second guess.

Diana stayed close to my side, abnormally so, with the scissors held against me. Gil looked at us strangely, but Diana didn't see his expression. She was concentrating on Marnie and Si who stood directly in front of us.

"What are you up to, Livvy?" Si asked, frowning.

"Oh, you found the scissors that belong on the props table. Very good. Just set them down. We need to rehearse the first act scene with the dance sequence," Marnie said. "Diana, be a dear…."

She didn't get any further before Diana shoved me aside and grabbed Marnie. Marnie shrieked and Si tried to attack Diana, who stabbed at him in the shoulder.

The police, already dealing with two men on the floor of the stage, hurried backstage to see what was happening. Inspector Dawson ordered Diana to set down the scissors.

She replied, "Stay out of my way while Livvy gets me the money that was Philip's."

"What? It's here?" Dawson said as Sergeant Mullins signaled his men to surround Diana and Marnie.

"I think so. I think it's in the storeroom by the stage door. The room Old Nick used. Old Nick is Philip Bernard's father." I hoped I was right and could find it quickly. I was feeling sweaty and weak.

"Go get it and bring it to me," Dawson said in a grim voice.

"This may take a little while. It's hidden well." I hurried past the aghast actors and crew members and into the storeroom. My side hurt but I didn't stop to look at it. Marnie was in danger and Diana seemed to have no qualm about killing.

I checked all the shelves. Nothing. I was breathing hard by the time I found that the work bench and the bins didn't have anything holding a clump of banknotes. I sat to go through the small sacks of nails and screws as sweat poured down my back. The ceiling was flat and too high to be easily reached, even if I'd had the strength to stand again. Then I checked the floor boards.

Old Nick was basically lazy. This had to be a spot easy to reach but unnoticeable by anyone not searching for Philip's money. I was getting hot and my side felt as if it were on fire. I stayed on the stool and looked around, pressing my palm into the spot that ached.

My hand felt sticky. I pulled it away to see it was covered in my blood. I looked around in a panic. I needed to find the money and get out of there so the police could stop Diana.

An old radiator was connected at both ends to pipes that went through the floor to connect it to the boiler that had to sit in the cellar. The boards where they were cut out for the pipe were short. I knelt beside the radiator and pried those boards up easily. Inside the space under one was a small tin box.

"Found it yet?" Sergeant Mullins asked from behind me.

"Got it." I rose and felt dizzy, grabbing the cold radiator to stay upright. The room was hot and I felt as if I were beginning to float. Strong arms caught me and helped me out of the storeroom and sat me on Old Nick's chair.

* * *

I was aware of a commotion in the backstage area, but nothing seemed as important to me in those next minutes as putting my head between my knees and breathing. Someone, a doctor judging by the bag I saw at my feet, poked at my side, making it burn more.

"She didn't hit anything important with those scissors, but the cut is deep and she's lost a lot of blood. She needs stitches. Transport her to the hospital."

When they went to put me on the stretcher, I tried to tell them I was fine, but my voice was far away and no one paid me any attention. The next thing I knew, I was lying down in a moving ambulance with Si sitting next to me.

"They'll be stitching us both up," he told me. "When they release us, I'll take you over to Marnie's. She's only two streets away."

"What happened to you?" At least I had enough strength to speak again.

"Diana swung the scissors and slashed my palm."

However, it wasn't to be, because when I told one of the nurses I was expecting a child, that not only got me sewed up more quickly, it put me on twenty-four-hour bedrest in the hospital. It was probably just as well, since I was hot and exhausted and couldn't have traveled a foot under my own steam.

I found I was allowed one visitor at a time when Marnie arrived. After three nurses fawned over her and told her how much they enjoyed her performances, she promised them autographs when the others came back to see me. "I can only stay a minute since Si and Gil and Nora want to check on you, too. How are you doing?"

"I've been examined by a doctor who says the baby wasn't hurt, but I must stop consorting with criminals for the rest of my pregnancy."

Marnie laughed before she became solemn. "Did you tell him it wasn't by choice?"

"That didn't seem to make any difference. What happened after I found Philip Bernard's money?"

"Diana attacked the sergeant, who stopped her and he put her in handcuffs. The inspector closed down the theater for today, getting us wonderful headlines. I'll show them to you when you are released."

"I imagine Si had a lot to do with those headlines." I gave her a grin.

"I imagine he did, too. I'll go now and send him back."

I saw as she left I was on a ward for eight with seven women in the other beds murmuring to each other, "That was Marnie Keller."

It wasn't Si who appeared next. It was my father.

Chapter Thirty

"Olivia, what are you doing here?" my father demanded, rather than asked.

"I was attacked by a crazy woman who killed or wounded several other people." I thought there might be safety in numbers when explaining this to my father.

"And my grandson?"

"So far, so good, according to the doctors."

"You need to quit working and go out in the countryside to live with your husband."

"Adam isn't in the countryside. He's on an army base somewhere working very hard to save our country."

"It can't be that far. And I know he's worried about you. He'll be here tomorrow to bring you to my house."

"Really?" I jerked upright and felt a stabbing pain in my side. "He wasn't supposed to be here until next weekend."

"I spoke to his commanding officer—"

"You did what?" My shriek attracted the attention of the other patients on my ward. Adam must have been furious with both my father and me for interfering with his work.

"And he gave Adam an immediate five-day pass."

"If all I have to do for him to get leave is end up in

hospital, then I'll have to fight with insane women more often." I gave my father a cheeky grin, which did nothing to improve his disposition.

"Olivia. I'll have you know this is not a joking matter, even if you have made the acquaintance of Marnie Keller." Despite his tone, my father looked starstruck.

"She's a lovely woman."

"I'm certain she is, but you need to stop endangering yourself. Think of my grandson."

"Apparently, the woman who attacked me was arrested, so I don't need to worry any longer."

"I don't think Adam will see it that way. You need to come home tomorrow and put your feet up. You're in a delicate condition." My father looked down at me lying in the bed as he frowned.

"I think Sir Henry is going to put me to work in an office where I will be far away from trouble."

My father sighed and shook his head. One of the older nurses came in and told him his time was up and he could visit me again tomorrow.

"Oh, I'll be back with her husband tomorrow. Maybe he can talk some sense into her." My father turned on his heel and marched out of the ward.

A moment later, Si came back to see me. He sat down on the chair by my bed and said, "The constable who was attacked by Diana is in this hospital, too, but he's not getting out tomorrow."

"Will he recover?"

"I think they are hopeful. We should know more by tomorrow, if they tell us anything."

"What about Old Nick?"

"He was poisoned, all right, with laudanum, but he was still alive when the police arrived. They brought him here and had his stomach pumped. He had no idea Philip Bernard had left his money in the storeroom."

"Then Philip Bernard recognized his father?"

"It's not clear yet, but I think Old Nick recognized his son and told him so."

"Does Old Nick get to keep the money? As his father, he must be his closest living relation." I was hopeful. Something good needed to come out of this tragedy.

"The money is being kept at Scotland Yard until they figure that out. I think Old Nick will get to keep it. And the poisoning has frightened him. He claims he won't drink anymore."

"Do you believe that?"

Si shook his head. "But we can hope."

"The drug was in his flask?"

"Yes. Diana promised him she'd fill it up with a good Scotch, but she'd laced it with laudanum. If he weren't so used to strong spirits, he'd be dead," Si told me.

"Will Diana, er, Carol Landry, stand trial for her crimes?"

"Yes, and you'll be called to testify. She'll be tried for killing her brother, Joe Landry, and attempting to kill you, the constable, and Old Nick. They don't have enough proof to try her for murdering Marshall Lowe, but they can only hang her once. And if they only get a conviction for her attempting to kill the three of you, she'll spend the rest of her life in jail."

"Or an insane asylum," I told him.

"You may be right."

"Is Old Nick keeping his job at the stage door of the Regent when he recovers?"

"Of course. The building manager, Art Jackson, likes him. I think the two of them originally came up with the black-market plan before Jane Barber and Michael Harris figured it out and demanded a share of the profits for their silence."

I raised my eyebrows at Si. "And somehow, everyone got away scot-free with the black-market scheme."

"Not at all. They captured the heavies with the goods, so they're all in jail. They all talked, so Jane, Michael, and Old Nick were all questioned. Somehow, no one mentioned Art Jackson. How do building managers get away with so much? And I don't know how he did it, but Old Nick explained away stabbing the heavy in the arm and his own involvement. I know where Philip got his talent as a playwright."

"How is everyone else and the play surviving all the excitement?" There was more I wanted to hear from Si.

"*Have You Seen My Mother-in-Law?* is shuttered permanently, but Bud Cosby has found backers for a new play, another comedy starring Marnie Keller, to rehearse here before going out on tour. Art Jackson is letting them rehearse at the Regent until he finds a new play to bring in."

Si was ordered out of the ward by the older nurse and he left me with a smile and a wave. A trainee nurse brought around our dinners, vegetable soup and toast for me, and I found that I was finally hungry.

The ward was settling down for the night when I heard the head nurse say, "Three minutes only." I glanced over and then smiled as I saw Sir Henry come up to the side of my bed.

"You certainly frightened Esther and me," he told me. "Has your father been by?"

"He wants me to sit at home and twiddle my thumbs."

"Not a bad idea, but perhaps we can find you a quiet job inside our offices. How about obits?"

"Sounds deadly," I whispered when I saw a nurse start over toward us.

Sir Henry rolled his eyes.

"Most of the time, the other reporters are complaining about my writing."

"Writing obits should focus all your skills, since they tend to be short, especially during a war with paper rationing. And I don't see how you can get yourself into trouble. The people you are writing about can't complain."

"Their families can," I reminded him. "And what if the deceased died under suspicious circumstances. Does that mean—?"

"No. No more investigating." He smiled at me. "This way you'll have your weekends free to visit Esther, so she can help you get the baby's layette together."

"But..."

He held up a hand. "I understand with all the rationing, this is a tricky business. She's had experience with what you'll be going through. You need her advice."

"You make it sound so ominous."

"I don't mean to. But I know Esther has said without her and James hiring cooks and nursemaids, and your help, she never would have survived. And that was before rationing."

"I won't have any help," I said with a sigh. What had I got myself into? I didn't know anything about being a mother.

"All the more reason for you to visit Esther and take lessons from her. Who knows? Maybe you can write a column on new motherhood for us."

The nurse came over and shooed Sir Henry out, leaving me with my thoughts and more worries than I had before.

* * *

I was dressed and ready the next day when Adam walked into the ward. Every female pair of eyes watched his handsome face and broad shoulders as he crossed the room on his crutches. The uniform only added to his male perfection.

After a long and lingering kiss, he said, "How are you?"

"We're both fine." I searched his eyes for any hint of blame that he'd had to find out our good news in such a terrible way. There was none.

Adam shook his head. "Your father talks as if the baby is his and mine. He doesn't yet seem to have figured out you have something to do with him."

"Or her?" I asked, raising my eyebrows.

Adam grinned. "Your father would never forgive us."

When I went to rise, somewhat stiffly, Adam gave me his

arm while balancing on his crutches. "You do that very gracefully now," I said.

"Lots of field practice with these things. I don't only teach in the classroom," he told me.

"Any chance...?" I asked.

"Only barracks housing," he said. "There is nothing out there. All the married men have been trying with no luck."

"Then I am doomed to write obits until my time is due."

"Sir Henry's new assignment for you? Good. It sounds safe."

"If it gets too dull, I'll write

"Livvy." Adam looked scandalized. one for my father and insert it in the morning paper."

"I'm joking."

"When am I to become a father?" His tone was still completely serious.

I waited to answer until we negotiated the stairs to the ground floor. "Late February is the best guess."

"I'll try to get leave. Chances are I won't be there. Will you forgive me?"

"Of course. Hitler is another matter. He doesn't get forgiven for a terrible breach of etiquette."

"Messing with my schedule?" he asked. He sounded a little uncertain about how to face parenthood or my comments.

I suspected everything would fall to pieces, so I'd decided to laugh at all the problems we'd face. It would all work out, our child would grow up healthy in a world no longer at war, and my father, the baby, and I would find a way to live in harmony.

Well, maybe not the last.

Despite my sore side, bandaged up where Diana had stabbed me, I happily traveled back to my father's house with Adam. Adam had leave and we had a lot to talk about. A lot of time to make up for. A lot of future to dream of.

And some names to consider.

I hope you've enjoyed Deadly Performance.

If you have, please be sure to read the rest of Olivia's adventures in The Deadly Series. And go to my website www.KateParkerbooks.com to sign up for my newsletter. When you do, you'll receive links to my free Deadly Series short stories you can download from BookFunnel onto the e-reader of choice.

If you want to let others know if you found Deadly Performance to be a good read, leave a review at your favorite online retailer or tell your librarian. Reviews and recommendations are necessary for books to be discovered and to get good ratings. Thanks for your help on behalf of all good books.

Notes and Acknowledgments

As soon as Britain declared war in WWII, the government closed down all the theaters to eliminate large gatherings that could be targets for German bombers. Within a few weeks, the Ministry of Defense (MOD) saw how necessary theaters were to civilian morale. Plays that were performed on the West End, however, also needed to be taken to cities up and down the country on tour. Some performances were taken to military bases, factories, and even down into the mines in an effort to keep up morale while Germany was bombing Britain and the blackout kept the streets dark. West End and other area plays were scheduled to conclude in time for the audiences to get home before the blackout began.

Blithe Spirit, Lady, Behave, and *Shakespeare in Southwark Park* were all actual plays performed in London in July of 1941. *Have You Met My Mother-In-Law* and the Regent Theatre are composites of theaters and plays from that time, with some lethal additions. Apparently, theaters in London had a habit of burning down and being rebuilt on the same site, creating basements and tunnels that had been opened up in places by German bombs. This makes possible the action near the end of the story.

The Stage newspaper, a weekly printed in London on Thursdays, was an excellent source of information for what was happening onstage throughout the country and the conditions the actors worked under during World War II as well as Ministry of Defense regulations for the theater.

Divorce was still extremely difficult for women to obtain before WWI. Options were widened in the 1930s to closer to modern rules, but society was still very prejudiced against divorced women. Marnie Keller, as a performer and public figure, would have wanted to keep that quiet.

Theaters in the West End today are not a great deal changed from WWII. If you get the chance to visit London, be sure to take in a play during your visit.

I'd like to thank my first reader, my daughter Jennifer, my editors, Elizabeth Flynn and Les Floyd, my proofreader Jennifer Brown, my formatter, Jennifer Johnson, and my cover artist, Lyndsey Lewellen. Their help has been invaluable in making this book as good as it can be. All mistakes, as always, are my own.

I thank you, my readers, for coming along with Olivia on this journey to the West End. I hope you've enjoyed it.

About the Author

Kate Parker grew up reading her mother's collection of mystery books by Christie, Sayers, and others. Now she can't write a story without someone being murdered, and everyday items are studied for their lethal potential. It had taken her years to convince her husband she hadn't poisoned dinner; that funny taste was because she couldn't cook. Her children have grown up to be surprisingly normal, but two of them are developing their own love of literary mayhem, so the term "normal" may have to be revised.

For the time being, Kate has brought her imagination to the perilous times before and during World War II in the Deadly Series. London society resembled today's lifestyle, but Victorian influences still abounded. Kate's sleuth is a young woman earning her living as a society reporter for a large daily newspaper while secretly working as a counterespionage agent for Britain's spymaster and finding danger as she tries to unmask Nazi spies while helping refugees escape oppression.

As much as she loves stately architecture and vintage clothing, Kate has also developed an appreciation of central heating and air conditioning. She's discovered life in Carolina requires her to wear shorts and T-shirts while drinking hot tea and it takes a great deal of imagination to picture cool, misty weather when it's 90 degrees out and sunny.

Follow Kate and her deadly examination of history at

www.kateparkerbooks.com
And www.facebook.com/Author.Kate.Parker/
And www.bookbub.com/authors/kate-parker

www.ingramcontent.com/pod-product-compliance
Lightning Source LLC
LaVergne TN
LVHW021234080526
838199LV00088B/4347